waiting

Women Writing Africa

A Project of The Feminist Press at The City University of New York
Funded by The Ford Foundation and the Rockefeller Foundation

Women Writing Africa is a project of cultural reconstruction that aims to restore African women's voices to the public sphere. Through the collection of written and oral narratives to be published in six regional anthologies, the project will document the history of self-conscious literary expression by African women throughout the continent. In bringing together women's voices, Women Writing Africa will illuminate for a broad public the neglected history and culture of African women, who have shaped and been shaped by their families, societies, and nations.

The Women Writing Africa Series, which supports the publication of individual books, is part of the Women Writing Africa project.

The Women Writing Africa Series

ACROSS BOUNDARIES
The Journey of a South African Woman Leader
A Memoir by Mamphela Ramphele

AND THEY DIDN'T DIE
A Novel by Lauretta Ngcobo

CHANGES
A Love Story
A Novel by Ama Ata Aidoo

COMING TO BIRTH
A Novel by Marjorie Oludhe Macgoye

DAVID'S STORY
A Novel by Zoë Wicomb

HAREM YEARS
The Memoirs of an Egyptian Feminist, 1879-1924
by Huda Shaarawi
Translated and Introduced by Margot Badran

NO SWEETNESS HERE
And Other Stories
by Ama Ata Aidoo

THE PRESENT MOMENT
A Novel by Marjorie Oludhe Macgoye

THE RAPE OF SITA
A Novel by Linsey Collen

TEACHING AFRICAN LITERATURES IN A GLOBAL LITERARY ECONOMY
Women's Studies Quarterly 25, nos. 3 & 4 (fall/winter 1998)
Edited by Tuzyline Jita Allan

YOU CAN'T GET LOST IN CAPE TOWN
A Novel by Zoë Wicomb

ZULU WOMAN
The Life Story of Christina Sibiya
by Rebecca Hourwich Reyher

LaPorte County Public Library
LaPorte, Indiana

waiting

GORETTI KYOMUHENDO

With an Afterword by M.J. Daymond

The Women Writing Africa Series

The Feminist Press
at the City University of New York
New York

B12600040

Published by the Feminist Press at the City University of New York
The Graduate Center, 365 Fifth Avenue, New York, NY 10016
www.feministpress.org

First Feminist Press edition, 2007

Copyright © 2007 by Goretti Kyomuhendo
Afterword copyright © 2007 by M.J. Daymond

All rights reserved.

No part of this book may be reproduced or used, stored in any information retrieval system, or transmitted in any form or by any means, electronic, mechanical, photocopying, recording, or otherwise, without prior written permission from The Feminist Press at the City University of New York, except in the case of brief quotations embodied in critical articles and reviews.

Library of Congress Cataloging-in-Publication Data

Kyomuhendo, Goretti, 1965-
Waiting / Goretti Kyomuhendo ; with an afterword by M.J. Daymond. -- 1st Feminist Press ed.
p. cm. -- (The women writing Africa series)
ISBN-13: 978-1-55861-541-0 (lib. bdg.)
ISBN-10: 1-55861-541-5 (lib. bdg.)
ISBN-13: 978-1-55861-539-7 (pbk.)
ISBN-10: 1-55861-539-3 (pbk.)
1. Uganda--Fiction. 2. Domestic fiction. I. Title.
PR9402.9.K96W35 2007
823'.914--dc22

2006033102

This publication is made possible, in part, by grants from the Rockefeller Foundation and the National Endowment for the Arts.

Printed on acid-free paper by Transcontinental Printing
Manufactured in Canada

13 12 11 10 09 08 07 5 4 3 2 1

With gratitude and love for Sandra Barkan in making it all possible

acknowledgments

I acknowledge the financial assistance of The Prince Claus Fund for Arts and Culture Development, which enabled me to complete this novel. My deepest thanks go to my supervisor, Professor Margaret Daymond, for her patience, understanding, interest, guidance and personal commitment to my work. I also wish to thank Professor Michael Green for having introduced me to the programme of creative writing at the University of KwaZulu-Natal, Durban.

I will remain forever indebted to my friends and family who allowed me the space, facilities, and time that I needed so badly to complete this novel: my sons, Mugema Gonzaga-Gonza and Baguma-Bantu, for understanding that I had to go away for nearly two years to write, and my mother for taking care of them. Thanks also to Godfrey and his family in London for the warm reception, for the five weeks at his house that were critical for me to meet my publisher's deadline; to Bernard Tabaire for keeping a wonderfully stocked library, my source for the research of this novel; and to the women at FEMRITE, the Ugandan Women Writers Association, for the sisterhood. In a special way, also, many thanks to Irene Staunton and Violet Barungi for their editorial advice, and Ayeta Wangusa for providing the Kiswahili words in the novel. I cannot forget my friends in Durban who encouraged, supported, and gave me company while writing this novel: Margaret and Ronald, Corinne and Angela, Chepkorir and Mbongiseni, Dr. Kwame, Rogier Courau and the families of the Plints, the Zulus, and the Mubangizis.

And the first will be last: This project would not have been possible without the generous support of my two great personal friends, Sandra Barkan and Carol Sicherman, to whom I remain forever grateful.

The year is 1979. Ugandan exiles and the Tanzanian Army, known simply as "the Liberators," combine to oust Uganda's dictator-ruler, Idi Amin, whose murderous regime has exterminated half a million people through state-sponsored violence.

part one

one

It was Saturday evening. Tendo was perched high up on one of the inner branches of the big mango tree, which threw hazy shadows over the large compound. Its leaves trembled despite the lack of wind, and one wafted slowly down from the branch and fell before us.

"It's announcing a visitor," Kaaka said, picking up the leaf and turning it slowly over in her hand. "A visitor who comes from far away, and has no intention of returning–like the leaf."

Suddenly, a whistle rang out from the mango tree. Startled, we all looked up expectantly.

"What is it, Tendo?" Father asked sharply, nervously.

"Nothing," Tendo answered with a light laugh. "Nothing," he repeated as if we had not heard him the first time.

We were all eating our evening meal in the yard between the main house and the kitchen. Mother pushed away her plate. Kaaka turned and looked at her.

"You must finish that food," she said tersely. "You'll need energy to push out that child . . . or," she paused, "to run."

"I don't like it," Mother answered, with a sigh. Her legs were stretched out in front of her and she shifted constantly from side to side, trying to find a position in which she could be comfortable. "Potatoes give me such heartburn and beans make me break wind the whole night . . . !" She pulled a face.

We all laughed, except Father, who looked at her as if she had given away what he would rather have kept secret.

"It's not the food," Kaaka said. "It's because the baby you are carrying has a lot of hair. That's what is causing the heartburn."

The sound of a plate hitting the ground made us all jump.

"Tendo!" Father shouted. "What is with you today? Did you have to throw that plate? Couldn't you have climbed down with it? Is that the way you thank the people who have worked hard to prepare a meal for us?"

"But you told me not to come down, Father!" Tendo answered, defensively. "I'm supposed to . . ."

"I know bloody well what you're supposed to be doing! And will you stop scaring us unnecessarily?" Father looked as if he would have hit Tendo if he'd been within reach. Maya reached over and picked up the offending enamel plate. Tendo had wiped it clean with his tongue. Maya looked at me sideways and we giggled.

"At least he has eaten his food," Kaaka said in a placatory tone. "No one seems to be eating these days. I've told you again and again, if these men come, they'll kill you unless you have enough energy to run, and run fast."

"What about you, Kaaka?" Maya asked her. "Won't you run?"

"Me?" she answered, pointing at her chest with the thumb of her right hand. "Me, I am not going to run away again. I will stay right here. At my age, what I have seen, I have seen. What I have eaten, I have eaten."

The sky was beginning to darken with gloomy gray clouds, swelling, racing, and dissolving into each other. The sun had hidden its face in fear of the angry clouds. Wind whistled through the coffee and banana plantations, and the bushes were violently shaken.

Mother had stretched out on the mat and begun to doze. Her nostrils opened and closed like the gills of a fish. The hollow at the base of her throat rose and fell rhythmically. Father sat down on the low, round stool, a small square table before him. A plate and bowl contained his half-finished food.

"Maya," Kaaka said, "collect the plates and wash them. You must get ready to leave before it starts raining.

". . . What!" she added, looking at Maya's plate. "You did not eat your food either. How many times . . ."

"My stomach is full, Kaaka," Maya said, lifting the blouse to expose her midriff. "I've eaten many jackfruits today. And papaws. And mangoes. And avocados. And . . ."

Kaaka waved her hand to silence her.

"Okay," she said, "that's enough. Now hurry up with the plates."

The clouds were moving at a more leisurely pace and seemed undecided whether to release their waters or not. Tendo climbed down from his tree. Mother rose slowly, sighing as she did so. "Maya, bring me my sleeping things," she said. "I think it is time to go."

Father returned from the house, a panga in one hand, a blanket and a long, heavy coat in the other. He stood looking at Mother for some time. Tendo, released from his cramped position in the tree, stretched his legs and flexed his hands, as if readying himself for a fight.

"Get the spear," Father told him. Tendo did not obey, but stretched himself again, luxuriously. "Bring the one at the foot of my bed," Father added impatiently. Tendo made a face, as if to say that he had already done enough for one day.

I started collecting the things that were lying about in the yard. I put the garden tools and other sharp implements in the store and locked it—just in case they came tonight. Earlier, Father had collected the goats from the bush, and they were safely locked in their pen. Maya was running back and forth, carrying the washed plates to the main house.

Darkness was gathering. Kaaka had already gone to her house, which was to the left of the main house. Maya came out carrying Mother's sleeping things: a mat and two blankets folded together and tied with a sisal string. Father walked ahead. He had tucked the heavy coat under his arm. Tendo held the spear while I carried the sleeping blanket that I would share with Maya.

Our sleeping place was a short distance from the house on the edge of the banana plantation where smaller trees had formed a dense little forest. It was in the midst of this thicket that we had cleared the grass for laying out the mats we slept on. The banana trees shielded the thicket from view.

The people we shared the hideout with had already arrived: Nyinabarongo, Uncle Kembo (Father's younger brother), the old man, and the Lendu woman, whose husband had gone to their home country, Zaire, to catch fish that he then sold in the market. Nyinabarongo had already spread out her two mats and her child sat on one of them, eating a roasted cassava. Mother greeted her and inquired after her child.

"She's fine, thank you," Nyinabarongo answered before asking where Kaaka was. "She's tired of packing up her blankets every day and sleeping here in the cold," Mother replied.

"But suppose they come tonight?" the Lendu woman asked, concerned. She was a woman of slight frame, but with a firm and compact body. When she walked, she seemed to bounce off the ground like a ball.

"I don't blame the old woman," Mother went on, shrugging her shoulders. "I don't see much use in my coming out here either. I can't run. They would still kill me if they found us here."

Nyinabarongo handed a cup of water to her child. The child shook her head. "The cassava will choke you," Nyinabarongo warned, but the child was adamant. She threw away the piece of cassava and started yawning. Nyinabarongo picked her up and held her on her lap, covering her with a blanket. The child was soon asleep.

Father opened the foldaway chair he had carried and leaned it against a tree trunk some distance from where we sat. He beckoned to Tendo to give him the spear and he plunged it into in the soft ground beside the chair. Then he folded his heavy coat and placed it on the back of the chair.

"Uncle Kembo and I are going to scout around first," he told us. "Tendo, whistle if you hear anything." But Tendo had already stretched out on the mat, his head covered with a blanket. He grumbled that he was exhausted from the sentry job he had to do every day.

Maya was massaging Mother's back with the strong balm Father had brought with him from the city. Its smell floated towards us and the child sneezed. I turned my head away, covering my nose and mouth with my palm.

"Is it helping?" Maya asked, pressing harder.

"Maybe," Mother answered. "Press harder. Use your fingertips, not your whole hand." Maya did as she was told, and Mother gave a soft moan.

"Ouch! Maya, be a bit gentle. What's wrong with you?"

Maya laughed lightly and continued massaging, adding more cream as she did so.

After some time, Uncle Kembo and Father returned. They continued talking in low tones, standing near their chairs. Uncle Kembo was wearing his heavy black coat, the belt firmly tied around his waist. He'd once been a night watchman at the sawmill, and I thought he looked like one right now.

The Lendu woman was lying on her mat, using a flattened banana stem to pillow her head. But she was not asleep. The old man had not carried a mat so he wrapped a blanket around his shoulders and leaned his back against a banana tree. Mother was breathing through her teeth, which made her sound like a saucepan sizzling on a fire. Nyinabarongo placed her child on the mat. The little girl stirred slightly but did not open her eyes.

Maya had rolled her entire body in the blanket and was lying near Mother. She had fallen fast asleep, and I had to shake her several times to wake her.

"Roll over," I whispered in her ear, not wanting to wake Mother. "What do you think I am going to use to cover myself? My bare hands?"

"But the ground is hard and wet!" She whimpered. I ignored her remark and pushed her to one side. Quickly, I pulled the blanket out from under her before she could roll over again.

The moon rose at eight. The child lying in her arms seemed larger as I gazed at her through the banana leaves. I could see only part of the child and her mother. She wanted to tease us, of course, unveiling her beautiful face shyly, slowly, as she did when wooing her husband, Sun.

"Is it true Sun made Moon pregnant and denied responsibility when the child was born?" I asked Nyinabarongo.

"Yes," she answered. "There are actually two children. If you look closely you will see the second one. Moon was very upset. That is why she runs away from Sun every time he tries to catch up with her to apologize. By the time he rises in the morning, Moon has already disappeared. At times she doesn't appear at all.

"I have a bad feeling about Kaaka," Nyinabarongo continued, changing the subject. "Suppose they come tonight. She should be here with us." She sounded tired. Her lower lip trembled as she spoke. She shivered in the cold air. "I wonder how long we will continue running." After a pause, she spoke again. "Look at your mother. Poor woman! She's heavy with child and should be sleeping comfortably."

I knew she wanted to talk, so I said, "She'll be all right. She's strong. It's your child I'm worried about."

"She will be fine. If only your father would allow us to make a small fire! But he insists that it will attract them here, which is nonsense! If they want to find us, they will find us."

Nyinabarongo had come back to live with her mother about two years ago after her husband's family had driven her away. The problem started with the birth of her first child, a boy, who had presented his legs first during a difficult childbirth. That is why he was given a twin name and various rituals were performed. When she bore her second child, a daughter, she was also given a twin name because the child's two upper teeth grew before the lower ones. That's how Nyinabarongo got her name, meaning "mother of twins," even though her children are not really twins.

As part of the rituals following the birth of twins, Nyinabarongo's husband's family invited her mother and two sisters for a meal. They were supposed to reciprocate, but her mother was ailing and poor. Then it was said that the twins were annoyed and had reacted by burning people in Nyinabarongo's husband's family. One of his brothers developed a pink smear on his nose and hands. So they chased her away, saying that she could return when her family was ready to invite them for a meal. But since then her mother had died and her two sisters had married and lived in other villages. So Nyinabarongo returned to her mother's house with the younger child, leaving her son behind. She always lamented about how much she missed her son, wondering if he was well, or if he had eaten.

I stretched out on the mat and tried to sleep. The stars were blinking down on us. It was very cold, and the blanket was not warm enough. I could hear Uncle Kembo and Father talking, but I could not see them. Everyone else seemed to be asleep, except the Lendu woman, who was tossing uncomfortably under her blanket.

The birds' morning conversation woke me up. Father, Uncle Kembo, and the Lendu woman had already gone. Nyinabarongo was tying the child to her back, her two mats already folded. Maya and Mother were walking towards the house. I jumped up and followed them. Father was already in the bathroom enclosure, and he shouted his greetings to us.

"You use so much water," Mother commented, looking down at the soapy water, forming rivulets as it ran out from the enclosure into the compound. "Don't you have any mercy on the people who fetch it?"

"The pipe must be blocked," Father shouted back, showing his head above the wooden railings. "It's not channeling the water into the hole, and that's why it appears to be a lot."

Kaaka made her way towards us, leaning her body on her walking stick. Her big stomach was visible through the long, loose dress she was wearing, and she seemed to be pushing it in front of her as she walked. She used her walking stick to hit a banana-fiber ball out of her way, and it rolled towards us before falling into the water streaming out of the bathroom enclosure.

Father came out of the bathroom, a towel wrapped around his waist, and inquired about Kaaka's night.

"I slept well," Kaaka replied. "But why are you bathing so early in the morning?" she asked him.

"I'm going to the Center to try to get some news," he replied. "I want to know what's happening in the city."

"But so early in the morning!"

"It's not that early," Father protested. "Look, the sun is already up."

"But won't you eat first?"

"When I come back. I want to catch people before they go their separate ways."

"But what ways can they go? Today is Sunday, and the churches are not open. All the priests are in hiding."

"They go to the beer clubs," Father laughed briefly.

two

We had learned about the details of the war a month before, when Father returned from the city where he had worked at the Main Post Office as a clerk. He told us that President Idi Amin was about to be overthrown by a combined force of Ugandans who lived in exile and the Tanzanian soldiers who were assisting them. The soldiers were advancing quickly, heading for Kampala from the southwestern border that Uganda shared with Tanzania. The districts along that route were already in the hands of the Liberators.

Amin's soldiers were looting shops, hospitals, banks, and private homes in the city. They wanted to seize as much as they could before the Liberators arrived. Some were fleeing towards the West Nile and Northern Ugandan regions, their home areas. People had vacated the city in fear of both the advancing Liberators and the fleeing soldiers. No one knew what each group was likely to do to civilians.

Our district was situated on one of the highways that led, via Lake Albert, to the West Nile and northern regions, and so, Amin's soldiers were using it as their exit route. And they had come in large numbers, invading the town of Hoima, looting, and killing people at night. The bush and banana plantations were the safest places to sleep, and during the day most homes posted a sentry in a tree to watch out for the soldiers. All shops, churches, schools, banks, hospitals, and police stations were closed, and most people had retreated to the villages, which were much safer. The soldiers, who felt they had nothing more to lose as the Liberators approached, had taken over Hoima town and had set up roadblocks from which they attacked people trying to move from one location to another.

Riding his bicycle at breakneck speed, Father sped back from the Center.

"We must dig a pit immediately," he informed us. "Last night they invaded five homes near the Center and stole everything of value. Luckily, the families were sleeping in the bush, otherwise they could have killed them too. But everything was taken—*everything*. Now we must hide whatever we own that's of value."

He was speaking breathlessly and gesturing like an actor. He asked Tendo to fetch the spade and the pick, saying that they would dig the hole a little distance from the sleeping area where the trees and shrubs were thicker.

By midday, the red soil that Tendo had scooped out from the pit as Father dug had formed a large mound like an anthill. Kaaka lit a big fire to soften the banana leaves that would be used to line the pit.

By evening, we were ready to take our most valuable possessions to the pit: the bicycle—which Father had dismantled—our mattresses, the radio, the saucepans, and our best clothes. We covered them with mats and goatskins, then we placed two old corrugated iron sheets on top.

That night we did not go to the sleeping place. Mother's back was hurting badly, and the balm did not soothe it. Father did not want to leave her alone in the house. He would go out every now and then to scout for soldiers before returning to his fold-away chair beside Mother. I had been sent to tell Nyinabarongo that she should come and sleep at our house; the Lendu woman was to go to Uncle Kembo's house.

Nyinabarongo and I walked back to our house together. I

carried the little girl, and Nyinabarongo carried her sleeping things.

"Did you hide all your valuables in a pit?" she asked, as we walked along the small path from her house to ours. The dew from the spear grass felt cold on my legs. Threads of smoke rose from the grass thatch of the Lendu woman's house.

"Yes, almost everything. What about you?"

"I hid only the mattress and a blanket. I dug a shallow pit. I hope they will be safe. The termites could eat them, you know."

We reached the house. I undid the cloth I had used to tie the child on my back and she slid down to the ground. She seemed weightless! Like a waif. My shoulder felt damp where she had rested her head.

After we had eaten, we went to bed. Kaaka came to sleep in our house in case Mother needed her during the night, and slept in the small bedroom I usually shared with Maya. Nyinabarongo laid her sleeping things on the floor there too. She placed the child on the mat and covered her with the piece of cloth that I had used to carry her. Tendo slept in the sitting room, and Maya and I slept in his room. We could hear Father moving about—going out and coming in again. He did not sleep much, though he had said he was very tired from digging the pit.

three

Another child had been born between Maya and me, but she had died of measles when she was two-years-old. I was about four at the time. Mother used to smear her with red soil from the anthill and put her in a dark room so that the measles would not affect her eyesight. Mother said that if she had been immunized, she might have survived. But there were no vaccines. The hospital always said they were out of stock. I had also suffered from measles, and so had Tendo.

"Come and get it for me," Maya was calling me. Her hands were stretched upwards, and she was standing on her tiptoes.

"Is it my fault that you're too short?" I asked.

"I'm not too short. It's because I'm still young, much younger than you!" she replied, her tone accusing. "Please!" she begged me. Her legs were stretched so tight that the veins stood out. Mother often laughed and said that Maya's legs were growing shorter as she grew older. When she was born, they were the longest legs anyone had ever seen, and Kaaka named her *Maguru-Maya*—legs of an ostrich.

I jumped up and plucked a mango from a low branch and handed it to her. Then I jumped again and plucked another for myself. We ate the sticky yellow fruit in silence. Maya ate greedily, the juice flowing down her arm and dripping to the ground.

But she hardly lost a drop. She bent her arm and trapped the juice inside her elbow, then she leaned down and licked it like a cat.

"What are you thinking about?" she asked me.

"About our sister who died."

"Oh!" Maya said carelessly and without interest, since she had never seen the baby.

"Tendo was six then," I mused, "and Kaaka had already been living with us for some time. I don't remember exactly when she came to live with us. I think it was before I was born. But I do remember asking Mother if Kaaka was pregnant. Her stomach looked so big! But she only laughed and promised to tell me all about the old lady's big stomach when I was a bit older. Mother said she just walked into the house one day and declared that she had left her husband for good and had come to live with her nephew, our Father."

"Do you think Father brought us presents?" Maya asked, changing the subject.

"No, I don't think so. He wouldn't have had time to buy them. Remember he came home very quickly as he feared the soldiers would find him in his house in the city. He's worried that all his property might have been looted by now."

"But what about the things that were wrapped in the plastic bag?"

"Which things?"

"Don't you remember the bag he gave Mother when he got back, and she gave it to you to take to the pit?"

"I guess those are the baby's things."

"Which baby?"

"The one in Mother's stomach, silly."

"Oh! When do you think it will come out? Is it a girl or a boy?"

"I don't know," I answered to both questions. I hoped it would be a girl, so that we could give her the same name as the baby who had died. And I also hoped that it would be soon. Mother looked more tired each day.

When Father first came from the city, fleeing from the

soldiers, he said Mother looked anemic and wanted to take her to the hospital immediately. But the hospitals were closed. The nurses and doctors had run away, fearing for their lives. The soldiers had already been there and looted the medicines. They had forced the remaining nurses to dress their rotten, smelling wounds. Father had tried to get for Mother the pills that bring more blood, but had failed. He asked me to cook the red-leafed vegetables that were given to children with little blood, but Mother refused to eat them, saying that she had no appetite.

What was going to happen to Mother? I thought I should ask Father to force her to eat the vegetables. I remembered the science teacher telling us that pregnant women needed to have enough blood; otherwise, if they bled too much during childbirth, they might die.

Maya had finished the mango. She had sucked the seed of all its flesh. She threw it over the pine hedge, but it got stuck in the pine trees. She walked over to the hedge, retrieved the seed and threw it with exaggerated energy far away from the hedge into the cassava plantation near the house. Maybe another mango tree would sprout in the years to come.

I went and sat on the porch, which felt warm to my buttocks. The retreating sun threw elongated shadows over the sheltered space. I pushed the palms of my hands down hard on the concrete and, when I raised them again, the rough surface had dug red patterns into them. I showed them to Maya. "It's because I have enough blood in my body," I said, wishing I could transfer some of it to Mother. "Let me see yours." She hid her hands behind her back and backed away from me.

Presently, Tendo walked over to us. His hands were firmly in his pockets, and at fifteen he was beginning to walk like a teenager, lifting one shoulder and then the other. He removed his hands from his pockets and started punching the air, fists folded as in a mock fight.

"I'm ready for them," he said, continuing to punch the air with both fists.

"Who?" Maya asked.

"Who else? The soldiers."

Maya laughed. I laughed too.

"What's there to laugh about?" Tendo asked, pausing; his breathing coming in short gasps. "Father said they have guns, but a man has to be prepared for a fight. When do you think they will come?" He turned to look at me.

"I don't know. You should ask Father."

I could sense that Tendo was bored. Under other circumstances, he would not be here, talking to us girls. He would be with his two friends, our cousins, who were Uncle Kembo's children. They would be playing football, fetching water, or riding the bicycle. But the two boys had gone with their mother to visit her people. Uncle Kembo was alone for the time being.

I would normally have been with my friend from school, Jungu, but her family could not stay in their house in town where her mother sold vegetables in the market because it was not safe there. They must have gone to her mother's village, which was about three kilometers from our home.

When I first started school, I never talked. I was shy and timid and would not answer any questions in class. The teacher told me to ask my father to pay her a visit so that she could talk to him about me. But I told her that Father did not live with us, but stayed in the city where he worked. Mother had to go to the school instead. She was furious when I told her.

"You! What have you gone and done?"

I kept quiet because I did not know what I had done.

"I have enough troubles. You think looking after you kids is a joke with Father far away in the city? When you go to school, you must study and do nothing else."

I had never seen Mother so upset. I feared that she was going to hit me. However, she was relieved when she came to school, and the teacher told her that the problem was that I was too quiet. I was not making friends and not responding to questions in class. Mother told me that if I did not speak, my mouth would smell for the rest of my life and that no one would ever want to come near me.

I was seven-years-old then, and Jungu became my friend. She was as quiet as I, and all the other children seemed to avoid her. They teased her about her hair, which they said resembled the tassels of a maize cob. Her real name was not Jungu, but she was called that because she had mixed blood. She was half Indian and half black.

Friday was always a holiday because President Amin had declared it so. It was a day when Muslims went to the mosque. On Saturday, we would resume school and then rest again on Sunday. Jungu started coming to our home every Friday so we could wash our uniforms together. Our home was only a short distance, a little more than one and a half kilometers, from where she lived with her mother in the town.

The mission school we both attended was situated on the road that led from our village to the town, and, at times, Jungu spent the weekend at our home so we could walk together to school on Monday.

There was no soap in the shops at the time, so we would pluck papaw leaves and squeeze them until they produced thick, dark green juice that we would mix with hot water. The mixture produced foam just like soap.

Mother said she knew Jungu's mother because she used to live in our village. When Jungu was born, her mother was too ashamed to raise her, so she had tried to kill her. It was the time when Indians owned all the businesses in the town. This was before Amin chased them away. They also owned the coffee factory, the cotton mill, and the sawmill. They were very rich.

Jungu's mother had just lost her husband, who had worked in the cotton mill. Every day she went to the mill to collect the money that was her late husband's salary, and the manager kept telling her to come back the next day. A month went by like that and she still had not gotten the money. Every time she went to meet that Indian, she returned home tired and crying. After about three months her stomach grew big and round. She did not say who had made her pregnant, and she never got her money.

Then Amin chased away all the Indians from Uganda. He said they were stealing our riches, so they should go back to their own country, though many had no country to go to, as they had been born and raised in Uganda. The manager of the cotton mill went away with his family.

Jungu's mother delivered two or three months after the Indians left. No one saw her give birth. She did not go to the hospital or call the birth attendant to assist her. People just saw her at the stream where she had gone to wash her blood-soaked clothes. When they asked after the baby, she said that it had died. The police came a week later, looking for a woman who had been pregnant. They took her away. She had left the baby in a garden and covered it with a big clod of earth, but someone had discovered it that same day. She was not put in prison, but released so she could nurse her baby. She never lived in our village after that. Instead, she went to town, where she started selling vegetables in the market.

Mother asked me if Jungu had told me who her father was, and I said, "No, we have never talked about it." The children always teased her because when we were required to write our fathers' names on a form, or anywhere, she would write her mother's instead. Mother told me that people of mixed blood were short-tempered and could easily commit suicide. She said I should be careful with my friend.

four

During the night, Mother woke me up, complaining of pain in her back. For the second night in a row, we had not gone to sleep in the banana plantation. Mother had told Father that she was not going to run again. A month of sleeping in the cold was all she could take. Besides, the baby was due any time. She would remain in the house with Kaaka. Her back was hurting too much, and she needed to sleep on a soft mattress. Father said he could not leave them alone in the house, so we would all stay together. Now she wanted me to massage her with the strong-smelling balm.

"Maya is not gentle," she complained. I massaged her for about an hour and then told her I was tired.

"Bring me my slippers," she said after a while. "I want to go to the latrine." I retrieved them from under the bed. She tried to force her feet into them, but they were swollen, and the slippers would not fit. She abandoned the idea and asked me to open the front door. I stumbled over Tendo, who slept in the sitting room. He turned over but did not wake up.

"Are we going out alone?" I asked, alarmed.

"What is there to eat us? The hyenas are sleeping at this time of the night."

"What about the . . . ?"

"The soldiers? For how long shall we keep running away from them? I need to pass stool, and I can't do it in the basin. Come."

■ ■ ■

I opened the door.

It was not very dark. The moon was half hidden, her soft rays dancing over the tops of the trees. Mother walked behind me. I carried Father's flashlight, which kept flickering on and off. The batteries were low. The goat pen by the side of the kitchen was quiet. We reached the latrine, and Mother entered. I handed her the dim light so that she could see her way.

"There are no leaves," she said to me. "Do you think you can pluck some for me? Get them from that plant over there, those light green, hairy ones."

I plucked a handful of leaves. I could not see their color properly, but I felt their soft hairs brushing against my fingers. I pushed my right hand in at the entrance, keeping my face averted. She took them, wiped herself, and we went back inside.

"You've been to the latrine?" Father asked as we entered. "Why didn't you wake me?"

"Alinda took me," Mother answered.

I went back to our bedroom. Maya was snoring lightly. My feet felt cold. I dusted the soil from them and blew out the lamp. Then I climbed into bed and covered my head with a blanket.

I was awakened again by the sound of the door opening. I could hear Mother and Father talking outside. They were coming from the latrine again. Then we heard the sound of a gunshot. I heard Father telling Mother to hurry inside. There were more gunshots. Maya stopped snoring and lay still. She called my name and asked, "Are those gunshots?"

"Yes," I answered, my voice trembling. I felt like going to the latrine myself.

I could also hear Tendo fidgeting with the latch on the door that led from the sitting room to the tiny corridor. On the left of the corridor was the bedroom I shared with Maya. Opposite it was Tendo's room, which was now occupied by Kaaka. Father slept on the floor near the back door so he would hear the soldiers if they tried to enter the house from that entrance. Tendo guarded the front door.

I got out of bed and almost collided with Tendo, who was standing in the doorway. Father stood next to him.

"Get dressed," Father said to us. "Tendo, get the panga and the spear."

"What is it?" Kaaka asked from her room. "You've been going to the latrine the whole night. Has the time come?"

"It's the soldiers," Father answered. "I think they're coming. The gunshots sound so near." He sounded very calm and controlled, and this reduced my own fear somewhat.

Maya and I were fully dressed, standing in the small corridor. Tendo was holding the panga. Father motioned us into the sitting room. Tendo moved ahead and removed his sleeping things, folding them roughly and dropping them into the chair. Maya squatted in the corner, clasping both arms across her chest. She was shivering slightly.

There was a brief silence. Mother spoke from her room, "They seem to have stopped." We waited, not hearing anything. Kaaka was struggling to sit up. She called me to find her dress and slippers. The gunshots came again, rapidly, shaking the house. Maya screamed, and Father shouted at her to be silent. She ran to Mother's room. I stood still, holding Kaaka's dress until she beckoned me to sit on the bed. My legs were shaking.

"They are going to kill us this time," she whispered to me. "You should have slept in the banana plantation."

We heard footsteps outside. Kaaka cocked her ear. Her bed was close to the small window in the room. She looked at me and made signs for me to get under the bed. There was loud knocking on the back door. Father blew out the lamp and the whole house was in darkness.

"It's me, Nyinabarongo."

Father moved quickly to the door and opened it. A rush of cold air came in the house.

"Are you mad!" he hissed at her. "The soldiers are nearby. They could have shot you!"

"But I couldn't stay in the house alone!" she answered breathlessly. Her child was strapped to her back, her eyes were wide open.

"I told you to sleep here, but you did not listen to me," Mother said.

"Why didn't you go to the Lendu woman's house? It's much nearer," Father said.

"She's not there. She went to sleep at Kembo's house. That's where I went first. I knocked, but they refused to open the door, even when I told them it was just me and my child."

"Come and sit over here," Kaaka told her.

I moved to give her space. Moonlight seeped through the cracks of the front door, so we could see each other. She bent over and undid the cloth holding the child on her back. As she lifted her down, the child began to cry.

"Shut that child up!" Father hissed, sharply.

"Eh, you! Leave the woman alone!" Kaaka spat back.

"Do you want the soldiers to hear us?" Father continued less sharply. "Put a breast in her mouth."

"She's not breastfeeding anymore," Nyinabarongo answered. "But I will keep her quiet."

"Put her on the bed," Kaaka said, moving over to make room. "She must be frightened." Nyinabarongo sat on the bed and picked up the child, placing her near her breast. She covered her with the cloth she had used for carrying her. The child fell silent.

The shooting started again, louder than before. We could hear people talking outside, then heavy footsteps approaching. Father looked around at us. He grabbed the panga from Tendo and indicated with his thumb for me to go where Mother and Maya were. I moved across the room quickly. Mother was sitting on the bed motionless, holding her chin in her hands. Maya was sitting up in bed, looking about her anxiously.

"What can we do?" she asked me in a whisper.

The heavy footsteps rose and fell, then stopped at the front door. We heard people kicking at the reed enclosure that encircled our house until it gave way. Words were exchanged. We were all still. It seemed as though nobody was breathing. There was silence both inside and outside. Then the footsteps started moving away. We remained silent for a long time until their running boots and laughter faded into the distance.

five

After we had eaten breakfast, people gathered in our homestead. In addition to Nyinabarongo and her child, there were Uncle Kembo, the Lendu woman, and the old man, who only came to our house when Father was around. Mother did not like him. One reason was that they had quarreled over the piece of land he had given to the Lendu woman and her husband. Mother had said that she did not want to have foreigners, whose ways she did not know, as neighbors. But the old man had argued that the Lendu people were useful because they had rid the village of monkeys by eating them. Previously, people had woken up to find their potatoes uprooted and eaten by the monkeys.

Other people agreed with the old man, but Mother never changed her attitude towards him. She kept saying that he was "a dangerous man," and she never allowed us to go near his house.

Father asked me to make more tea, and Maya went to the garden to cut more maize. The fire had died down, and so I added two big logs. One log was still wet, and it produced a lot of smoke. I took it off and asked Tendo to split it into smaller pieces for me. Maya came back from the field with the maize cobs, and I started peeling off the husks.

"Don't you have eyes?" I asked her, annoyed. "Why did you cut the young ones?"

"Leave me alone. Why didn't you go and cut them yourself?"

"Then you'd have made the tea and this fire? Eh?"

The water was boiling. I uncovered the kettle and added tea leaves, measuring them with my palm. I also added herbs for flavor and covered the kettle again. "Bring the tray," I said to Maya. "And the cups."

I arranged the maize cobs near the firestones. The heat from the embers would roast the cobs till they turned brown. They started popping as the corn burst and a piece of the white substance landed on my forehead.

"You see," I told Maya when she returned, "you want me to lose my eyes. Next time, cut only the ripe ones."

I broke the two cobs that had already browned in half and placed them carefully on the plastic plate. Vapor collected at the sides. I placed the plate on the tray, covered it with another, and handed it to Maya.

"Are there enough cups?" I asked her.

"The Lendu woman has said she will not take tea. She has already eaten breakfast."

"Kneel down while you serve," I reminded her. She walked off sullenly.

"Eh, you girls! Are you measuring the size of the visitors' stomachs? Is the maize in the garden finished?" Father said to Maya, loud enough for me to hear.

"Alinda's roasting more," Maya answered.

"And bring one more cup for her. We can't eat while she just sits here and watches us," Father added, pointing to the Lendu woman.

"But she said . . ." Maya began, but Father silenced her. "Another cup," he said. Maya came back to the kitchen with the empty plate and held it out to me.

"Do you think I'm a machine?" I asked, crossly. "Put down the plate and collect the cups from Mother and Kaaka. They must have finished by now."

"How does that old man eat maize?" Maya whispered. "What happened to his teeth?"

"Keep your voice down," I hissed at her. "He'll hear you."

"But what happened to his teeth?"

"Ask Mother. Though she'll never tell us the whole story, not about that man anyway. Now go and . . ."

Father was talking to our visitors. The soldiers had also passed by their homes, but as with us, they had not bothered anyone.

"They are scouting around first," Uncle Kembo said. "But what do they want with us?"

"We don't have money," the old man added. "We're poor people."

"They have turned their shame into anger. If they want to fight, they should go to the city where the real fighting is. How can you fight people without guns?" Uncle Kembo asked.

"It's only our districts that haven't fallen to the Liberators," Father added. "That's why they're running to hide here, and terrorize us."

"But what are these so-called Liberators thinking?" Uncle Kembo spoke again. "How can they liberate just one part of the country? How do they expect us to defend ourselves?"

"The only thing for us to do is to sleep in the banana plantation. It's safer there. Last night was a wake-up call. Next time they will finish us off," the old man said, as if he were looking death in the eye.

Mother was calling me. She wanted to have a warm bath, but there was no water in the jerry cans. I called Tendo and asked him to go to the well and fetch two cans of water.

"I'm tired," he snapped.

"Shut up!" I shouted at him. "Mother wants to bathe. And I'm going to cook lunch. Besides, Father has said we are sleeping in the banana plantation tonight. So, I have to cook early."

When the water boiled, I poured it into a plastic bucket and carried it to the bathroom enclosure. Then I carried another half-full jerry can with which to cool the hot water. Mother came out of the house, walking slowly, with a *kanga* wrapped around her shoulders, a sponge and soap in one hand, and her slippers in the other.

"Bring me the stool," she said to me. "No, not that one. The low one." She sat with her legs stretched apart, her stomach sticking out. Her navel looked like a big, ripe pimple growing on her stomach.

"Pour a lot of water on my head. Yes. There." Her eyes were closed. "Okay, now go away. I have to wash myself." After a while she called me again. "Give me my *kanga*." She started drying herself, and I helped her to dry her back. There were bloodstains on the tip of the *kanga* she had used to wipe herself down. I drew her attention to them.

"You're bleeding?" I asked.

"My time is near," she said as a way of answering me. I tried putting the slippers on her swollen feet but failed. She walked bare-footed into the house. She sat on the bed and pulled a long, loose dress over her head. She did not put on underpants. I combed her hair, and she lay on the bed, groaning quietly.

"Cover me," she said to me. I went to our room and got an extra blanket.

"Do you want me to call Kaaka?" I asked.

She shook her head. "Go and prepare lunch," she said to me. "You're sleeping in the banana plantation tonight. You must eat early."

I went back to the kitchen and took down two ropes of meat that had been hanging above the fireplace for almost a week. I cut them into smaller pieces. They were tender and would not take long to cook. I put them in a saucepan with water, then added two big logs to the fire and started fanning the flames until they burst into bright yellow sparks.

I placed the saucepan on the fire and covered it with an enamel plate. Then I left the kitchen and looked around for Maya, but I could not see her. When I called out, she answered. She was sitting with Kaaka in the shade of the mango tree, talking to Nyinabarongo. "Come and peel the potatoes," I said.

"She's still removing my jiggers," Kaaka answered. "I don't know where these small parasites come from. I seem to be the only one they like. It must be that my skin is wrinkled and soft."

"They're not small, Kaaka," Maya said. "Look at this one," she added, holding up a big jigger, which was impaled on the tip of the safety pin that she was using to extract the parasites from Kaaka's fingers and toes.

"You must put paraffin in the holes where the jiggers have been," Nyinabarongo said, "otherwise they will grow into big wounds."

I returned to the kitchen and started peeling the bananas first and then the sweet potatoes.

"I thought you wanted me to do the peeling," Maya said, walking into the kitchen.

"You can pound the cassava."

"Eh, how many kinds of foods are we going to cook?"

"Just pound the cassava. You know Mother can't eat sweet potatoes, so I have to add bananas for her. And Father only eats millet for supper."

"But this is not supper. Where is Tendo? He ought to be helping us."

"Just pound the cassava!" I shouted, losing my patience. My nerves were frayed, and I was feeling nervous about the blood I had seen on Mother's clothes.

"Is this enough?" Maya asked after a time, holding out some dried pieces of cassava in a basket.

"It should be. So long as it is half the millet flour that we're going to mix with it." I struggled to sound calm.

"I can't find the sieve," she moaned.

I went out to pick fresh banana leaves in which to wrap the potatoes and bananas. The nearest trees had almost no leaves left on them, so I made my way further into the plantation. I was cross when I got back to the house.

"Is it you who cuts banana leaves like that?" I asked Maya. "If you cut off all the tender young leaves, how do you expect the tree to grow and produce fruit?" She kept quiet and continued pounding. She was kneeling in front of the mortar, raising the pestle high up with both arms, then bringing it down with exaggerated effort. I could sense she was anxious too. The ground beneath the mortar shook, raising a small cloud of dust. Cassava pieces flew out of the mortar, spreading on the floor, white like chalk.

After I had removed the spines from the banana leaves, I placed two leaves across each other in the saucepan, then I placed potatoes at the bottom, bananas in the middle, and green vegetables on top.

"How many foods are. . ." Maya had stopped pounding and was watching me in amusement.

Kaaka came and stood in the doorframe, her big stomach protruding in front of her.

"How will you mash the bananas?" she asked. "You haven't tied them with banana fibers."

"I'm not going to mash them. Mother wants to eat them as fingers."

"Is she still sleeping?"

"Yes. She said the time is near. There was blood on her dress this morning."

"Blood! That is not a good sign," Kaaka said. "Have you told your father? Where is he, by the way?"

"I don't know," I replied. "He must be with Tendo. I think they have gone off with the visitors who were here this morning."

"But it's almost noon. They should be back by now. I'll go and check on your mother."

The meat was boiling.

"I don't like the smell of goat's meat," Maya said, holding her nose.

"The smoked one doesn't smell that bad, does it? Besides, this one was a female. It's the male goats that smell really horrible."

"Yes, and Mother says she smokes them to get rid of the smell. And why has Father decided to slaughter all the goats? Every day we eat meat. It's like Christmas!"

"Don't be foolish. Don't you know that if we run away the soldiers will come and eat them?"

"But he's only slaughtering the females."

"Yes, because there are only two males. One he is reserving for Mother if she produces a baby boy. The other is to make the other females pregnant."

Maya laughed out aloud. "How do you know all these things?"

"Because I'm not as foolish as somebody. And I'm older. You're only nine, so you wouldn't know about these things.

Check in the cupboard and get the groundnut paste. I think it's time to add it to the meat now."

There was only a little remaining in the tin. I used a spoon to scrape the sides and put it in a bowl. Then, I added the boiling stock from the meat, stirring it with a wooden spoon.

"It's going to be watery," Maya said. "And Father likes his paste very thick."

I continued stirring. It was too late to start pounding more groundnuts. We had to eat early. When the paste had completely dissolved in the hot stock, I poured it over the meat on the fire, and continued stirring.

"Can I add the salt now?" Maya had salt in her cupped palm and, before I could reply, she had emptied it into the meat.

"You!" I shouted.

"What? You think it's too much? I used the same amount Mother uses."

"It's not that. The paste will never thicken now. You always add salt last, just when you are about to remove the stew from the fire. Maya, you have to learn how to cook properly, now that Mother is not well. We have to take over the running of this house." I turned to look at her, and her face was grim.

When Father and Tendo came back, I put the water for mixing the millet flour on the fire to boil. The vegetables and meat were ready. Tendo came and sat on the chair in the kitchen, placing his elbows on the small table Father used when eating. The logs were beginning to produce a lot of smoke. Tears filled my eyes. I wiped them away with the hem of my skirt.

"What are you cooking?" Tendo asked.

"Are you blind?" I answered not looking at him. I would have to blow the fire with my mouth, since I could not find the fan.

"I'm only asking."

"Those who ask what they know are looking for laughter."

I found a plastic cup and used it to remove some boiling water from the saucepan on the fire.

"Why are you reducing the water?" Tendo was still on my

case. "I want to eat enough for both lunch and supper. You know we'll not eat again until tomorrow, and it's still only . . ."

"Stop it, Tendo!" I glared at him.

"Hey! Don't bite off my head. Everyone seems to be on edge today!"

"I'm only reserving some water in case the paste becomes too hard," I said slowly, trying to sound composed. I sprinkled a little flour in the boiling water. It bubbled violently. A small bubble jumped out and landed on my shin. I wiped it off quickly with the back of my hand. I poured in more flour and started stirring with the wooden stick.

I put the paste in the basket with a small cover, and we started laying out the food. Mother did not want to leave her bed to come and eat. Kaaka said she was vomiting and had asked us to keep her food until her stomach settled.

Darkness was beginning to fall. Father ate in a hurry. He said he was going to fetch the birth attendant. We hardly spoke as we ate. Everyone was tense. An uneasy feeling was beginning to settle in my stomach. We cleared away the eating things and put them in the cupboard.

Father had not been gone long before he was back, saying that he had met Uncle Kembo, who had told him that some soldiers had been sighted approaching the shops at the Center. Father had been unable to go to the birth attendant's house. He said he was going to call Nyinabarongo, but Kaaka stopped him.

"That woman behaves like a child. She wouldn't even know how to cut the cord. Anyway, what can you expect of a woman who let her in-laws chase her away from her own home?"

I was surprised by Kaaka's unkindness towards Nyinabarongo. I had never heard her talk of our neighbor like that.

"Then I will call the Lendu woman," Father said.

"That childless one! They say she has never fallen pregnant. What can she know about childbirth? Besides, she wouldn't know about our ways. I will attend to her myself."

"But you have no eyes! You cannot even remove your own jiggers!"

"I know what to do. I have delivered babies before. You take the children to the sleeping place before those men come. I will remain here with Mother."

"Maybe Alinda should stay with you," Father said, turning to me. "She can assist you." There were furrows of worry on his face, and for the first time since the war began, I detected signs of fear in him.

"I'll need a new basin," Kaaka said.

"Where do you expect me to buy a new basin now? All the shops are closed." Father was visibly angry. The vein on his forehead stood out, pulsating.

"Well, I'll need a clean basin. Don't worry. I'll use mine." Kaaka was insistent. "I hope she will be all right. Nowadays women go to the hospital! They're not used to our ways of delivering."

Father was silent. He turned to me. "Stay close to your mother. Come and call me if there is a problem. Maybe I'd better stay."

He was confused, torn by his different responsibilities. He paced in the yard, mumbling to himself. I did not know what to say or do that would make sense at this moment. The moon would be up late tonight. Each day she delayed her appearance longer, until she would stop coming out completely.

"You can't stay," Kaaka said calmly. She seemed to be the only one not afraid of what lay ahead. "You know they always kill the men first," she added. "It's too dangerous for you to be here with us."

"But what about you?" Father was becoming very agitated.

"Who, me? But I'm an old woman, and your wife is heavy with child. They won't bother us. Alinda will hide under the bed."

"No. Not there," said Father. "That's the first place they'll look!"

"Well, where do you expect her to hide?" said Kaaka crossly.

Mother called me from her room. I went to see what she wanted.

"I am in pain," she told me simply. "Are you going to the sleeping place?"

"I'm staying with you. The rest are going. Can I bring you your banana fingers?"

"No. I cannot eat now. Kaaka has already given me the enema."

She asked me to massage her back with the balm. She was lying on the mat, facing the wall. I pulled at the *kanga* she had covered herself with up to her waist. The area between her waist and shoulders was damp so I used the tip of the *kanga* to wipe away the sweat. Shafts of pain seemed to be running through her whole body. I applied a little cream and used my thumb to massage her. She started moving her head, grinding her teeth.

"Am I hurting you?"

She grunted and mumbled something I could not hear. "Stop," she said finally. "It's not helping."

Father came in and stood looking at her for some time. "We're going now," he said. "Come and fetch me if you need me."

I nodded. I was very worried about Mother. I felt hot tears burn my eyes, but I blinked them away. I did not want her to see me crying. But suppose . . . The uneasy feeling made my stomach rumble and my legs become weak. I sat on the bed. Kaaka came in and looked at Mother and said she wanted to check the position of the baby's head. She asked me to go out of the room. She had smeared shea butter on her fingers. I went and stood by the back door, listening to the noises of the night. When Kaaka called me back to the room, I found Mother lying on her back, her legs spread apart. Kaaka was rubbing her stomach, which seemed to loom above the rest of her body like a mountain.

"Go and wash my basin, properly, with a lot of soap and warm water," Kaaka instructed me.

When I brought it back a little while later, she told me to place it at the end of the mat where Mother was lying. I stood there, not knowing whether I would be needed now or later. When Kaaka did not say anything, I went and sat on the bed, waiting.

Mother continued moaning, and Kaaka massaged her stomach more vigorously, at times pressing on it. I stretched out on the bed and covered my feet with the dress that Mother had been wearing in the morning after her bath. I closed my eyes. My eyelids felt heavy and tired. I slept.

six

Kaaka was calling my name. I opened one eye. The yellow light from the lantern blinded me. Mother was whimpering softly. Her head was raised, and she seemed to be looking down over her stomach. "It's almost here," Kaaka was saying. "I can see the hair now. Big head." She called my name again, and I responded.

"Where are the baby things your father brought from the city?"

"In the pit," I replied.

"Go and get them, quick," she said, urgently.

"I'm afraid of the dark," I told Kaaka.

"It's almost morning! The cocks are already crowing. Your father is out there. Ask him to take you to the pit."

Mother let out a prolonged groan, pushing. Kaaka turned her attention to her and urged her to push harder. I stood up and wrapped Mother's dress around my shoulders. Then I moved to the door and opened it. Quickly, I stepped outside. I walked swiftly, noiselessly, the soft grass beneath my feet muffling the sound of my footsteps. The gentle light from the breaking dawn made the banana trees look like the silhouettes of soldiers standing to attention.

"Who is it?" Father's voice called out quietly but loudly enough to make me jump.

"It's me," I replied.

"How is your mother?" he asked anxiously. "Has the baby arrived? Is she all right?" He was whispering.

"The baby is almost out. I've come to fetch the baby clothes from the pit," I whispered back.

"Why ever did you put them in the pit? At times, you can be very stupid. You knew the baby was going to arrive soon." He sounded both excited and fearful. He removed the two corrugated iron sheets gently in order to make as little noise as possible. "Now, where are the clothes?" he whispered hoarsely, "I hope they're not right down at the bottom."

Silently, I pointed out the plastic bag, which was sitting on top, where Mother had told me to put it. Father picked it up and handed it to me; the soft light and the silence was broken only by the croaking sound of the frogs.

We had begun moving towards the house when we heard the gunshots. Their harsh barks sounded very close. Father pulled me to the ground, and I crouched beside him. More shots rang out from all sides. Father beckoned me to crawl closer to where the banana trees were at their thickest and would shield us from the light of the dawn. Heavy boots ran towards the house.

"God have mercy," Father whispered.

My heart was beating so loudly I thought the soldiers would hear it. I raised my head a little and saw six men in army uniforms walking towards the house. They were speaking loudly, and one of them raised his gun and shot into the air. I started to scream, but Father clamped his hand over my mouth and choked the scream back.

"I have to go and save your mother and Kaaka," Father whispered. He crawled a few paces forward. I crawled behind him, the plastic bag tight under my arm.

Father looked back and made an impatient gesture for me to stay where I was. He crawled a little further ahead. Daylight had now broken, and we could see the soldiers clearly. They were shouting, but I could not make out their words. It sounded as if they were speaking in another language.

Kaaka came out of the house. She seemed unafraid. Father

had stopped moving. Kaaka asked the soldiers loudly what they wanted. They all started talking at once, pointing their guns at her. More soldiers came. Kaaka told them urgently that she was in the process of delivering a baby, and she was needed back in the house.

The soldiers sounded agitated and dangerous, and I wished I could warn Kaaka to speak to them nicely. Father slowly rose to his feet. I could not believe it. Had we not been told that they would kill the men first? Fear seemed to freeze my mind. Again a soldier fired in the air. Father dropped to his knees. The soldiers advanced until about three or four of them stood in the doorway, shouting. Father seemed to understand what they were saying, and I heard him whisper something, his voice shaking.

"If you want food, I don't have any. If you want . . ." Kaaka's voice faded as the men simply pushed her aside.

The soldiers who had been standing in the doorway followed, and they all entered the house. Father cursed, regretting that Kaaka had talked him into sleeping in the banana plantation. I felt someone moving behind me and gasped. Uncle Kembo put his hand on my shoulder. "Shh," he said, "It's only me," and somehow I felt a little comforted that we were not quite alone.

One soldier seemed to be roughing up Kaaka. He shouted at her, and Uncle Kembo translated. "They want women, food, and money," he said, "and they want to know where everyone else is hiding." But Kaaka did not understand their language. Uncle Kembo said they were speaking in Kiswahili, a language mainly spoken by Amin's soldiers.

Kaaka laughed loudly, scornfully. "Do you have no respect?" she called out. "No shame? Pushing around an old woman, who is trying to deliver a baby?"

One soldier kicked her hard in the stomach. Kaaka screamed. Father stood up again, ready to move forward, panga poised.

Uncle Kembo spoke. "Don't be stupid. How can a man armed with a panga fight twenty men with guns?"

"But we have to do something!" Father hissed desperately.

Lying on the ground, Kaaka continued talking. "You want to kill an old woman like me? Go ahead then. What have I to fear?"

The soldier kicked her again. The three or four who had entered the house came out and started talking to those outside. Two had climbed into the mango tree, and its branches creaked under their weight. They began throwing the fruit down to their friends, who snatched them up and ate like monkeys. For a moment, the tension seemed to ease.

But the soldiers began to argue as they ate the mangoes and threw the seeds into the yard.

Uncle Kembo translated. "Some say they must search and find the owners of the home. Others are arguing that the house is empty with nothing of value to steal, so they should move on." Their loud voices sounded ugly as they echoed across the empty yard.

Kaaka slowly managed to sit up. The soldier who had assaulted her muttered something, and the other soldiers laughed as if they were drunk. Kaaka spoke again, "Go, you beasts! I have to attend to a woman giving birth to a baby who will be more useful than you. How can you beat a woman old enough to be your great-grandmother?

"Do you think you can scare me? Me, who used to beat my husband until he urinated in his trousers? Heeeeh," she laughed. "If you are real men, go and fight with your enemy, instead of coming here to terrorize a poor harmless old woman like me. Eh?"

"What's wrong with her?" Father was beside himself. "Only one of them needs to understand her, and she's dead!"

The soldier whom she had addressed pointed his gun at her and fired. Then he fired again, aiming at her stomach. The other soldiers had walked away; one who seemed to be their leader shouted at him to follow them. The soldier kicked Kaaka once more and she screamed loudly. Then he turned around and began to walk away. The sound of their footsteps beat loudly on the dry earth.

Father was standing, his arms lifted in despair and frustration. There was a movement behind me in the bushes, and the women joined us, Nyinabarongo's child clinging to her back. We heard the soldiers laughing in the distance, and then, finally, they were gone. We all stood up and started talking, breathless with anxiety. Uncle Kembo silenced us with a curt movement of his hand.

Father rushed forward into the yard, something like a groan escaping from his lips. Kaaka was covered in blood. He bent over her.

I was still clutching the plastic bag that contained the baby's things when I ran inside the house to find Mother.

seven

Mother was gasping, and calling out softly for help. I saw a cushion of blood, and heard a baby crying. Mother told me to find a small bundle under her pillow, which contained a razor blade and some cotton, wool, and gauze.

"Cut," she commanded, when I told her I'd found it.

"Cut what?"

"The umbilical cord."

My hands trembled, and I could not hold the razor blade steady. I could not see the cord. I feared to look at the jellied blood next to the baby. I thought I might vomit and tried hard to contain myself. Then I saw something like a fleshy string, coiling out of the bloody mess and winding its way to the baby's stomach.

I severed the cord. Nervously, too quickly. Only half of it was cut. It was thick, thicker than I had imagined. The baby was crying loudly. It had lots of hair, but it was covered in caked blood. Mother was commanding me to cut. I put the razor on the cord again and cut. Slash! It fell off.

She asked me to bring the clean basin I had washed the previous night, and put the afterbirth in it. I touched it gingerly, my hands still trembling. I tried to get hold of the afterbirth, but it slipped through my fingers and fell back towards the baby. It danced around in the pool of blood still seeping from Mother's womb, swimming like an egg yolk.

"Give me the baby," Mother told me. "Is it a girl?"

I was shivering so badly that I could hardly speak. I tried to hold the baby, but it was covered in slippery liquid. Mother pulled herself up into a sitting position and reached for the baby. She picked up the dress I had used to cover myself, and wrapped the baby in it.

"Don't throw the afterbirth in the latrine," Mother was talking to me. Her voice seemed distant and weak. I could see her mouth opening and closing, but I could not hear what she was saying. "Dig a hole and bury it there–deep, so the dogs don't find it and eat it." The words seemed to be falling from her lips.

part two

eight

Mother sings as she works. She is seated on a low stool, her legs crossed at the ankles. She is washing the plates and cups we used for last night's supper. She is singing the song of the doves:

Kade efokere kisato
(The calico has turned into a goatskin)
Kade efokere kisato
(The calico has turned into a goatskin)
Mujungu agambire kugyokya
(The white man has said he is going to burn it)
Mujungu agambire kugyokya
(The white man has said he is going to burn it)

I am seated next to her, holding the baby. He has refused to take milk because his gums are covered with weals. He is crying silently, his mouth opening and closing like a baby bird when it wants to drink water. I stand up and put him on my shoulder and start rocking him back and forth. His head dangles from his soft neck, and I quickly place my right hand at his nape to support him. Saliva, mixed with blood, dribbles from the corner of his mouth onto my dress.

Maya comes back from the well carrying the big earthen pot

on her head. She asks me to help her put it down. Stupid girl, can't she see I am holding the sick child?

"Ask Mother," I tell her.

"Mother is not here!" Maya yells at me.

But I can still hear Mother singing the song of the doves, which we had baptized "Kaaka's song" because she loved to sing it to us and narrate the story of its origin.

When the white people first came to our village, Kaaka was only a little girl, and small girls and boys never used to wear clothes. They would just cover their private parts with pieces of goatskin.

The white men ordered that all girls should wear dresses to cover their breasts and buttocks, but their parents were too poor to buy the ready-made dresses sold in the shops. Instead, they used calico to make wraps that the young girls wore for a long time. They never seemed to wear out—like goatskins. The white men became angry because the adults were not buying the ready-made dresses sold in their shops. One day, all the white men in the village gathered for a meeting and decided that the young girls should burn their calicos, so they would be forced to buy dresses.

A female dove was sitting in the branch of the tree under which the meeting was being held and heard this conversation. She started singing to the young women as they passed by on their way to the plantations in the morning, warning them that the white man was going to burn their wraps:

Kade efokere kisato
Kade efokere kisato
Mujungu agambire kugyokya
Mujungu agambire kugyokya

I can't hear Mother's voice anymore. A mist is rising in thin strands, swirling around the top of Kakundi hill. I can vaguely see Maya's figure moving about the yard. The mist begins to thicken, completely shrouding the mountain's top with layers of cloud. The baby starts to cry again, making buzzing sounds close to my ear, like a mosquito. After a while, the mist begins to clear, and I can now see the hilltop again and Maya's figure more clearly. But where is Mother?

nine

"You're dreaming!" Maya cried out.

I opened my eyes. The baby was lying next to me, crying silently, without tears.

"You're dreaming!" Maya said again, giggles choking her voice. "You're dreaming during the day!" she laughed aloud.

"It's not daytime," I said, pulling myself to a sitting position. A soft wind blew the lower part of the mat I was lying on, flipping it over. Small particles of soil fell into the baby's eyes and open mouth. I quickly pushed back the mat with my legs and wiped the dust from his face.

"It's evening already," I said, looking around me at the approaching dusk.

"You were singing in your dream!" Maya was watching me with amusement as she began laughing again.

"Shut up!" I shouted at her, putting steel in my voice. "Where's everybody?"

"And you were calling for Mother," Maya continued. A shadow of sadness fell across her face, and she stopped laughing.

Father came into the yard and walked over towards us. He looked down at the baby, then bent, and picked him up, holding him clumsily.

"How is he?" he asked, looking at me. "Has he drunk any milk?"

I shook my head as I picked up the piece of cloth that I had used to cover the baby and handed it to Father.

"Cover him, he will get cold."

"But this is wet!" Father said, holding the cloth near his nostrils, "and it smells of urine."

"It's not urine. It's the saliva coming from his mouth. Cover him," I said again.

Father looked at me hesitantly. He looked haggard, and his eyes stared blankly into space. His hands shook.

"Fold it and use the bottom part, which is dry," I told him.

"I think you'd better hold him," he said, handing me the baby. "Maya, bring me my foldaway chair. Where's Tendo?"

"He went to Uncle Kembo's house," Maya answered.

"He ought to be back! Have you prepared the evening meal yet?"

"No," Maya answered. "Alinda hasn't told us what to cook. She was sleeping the whole afternoon. She was even dreaming and . . ."

"Why do you wait to be told? Can't you see Alinda is minding the baby? You must help her, Maya."

"But the baby doesn't like me; when I hold him, he cries. He only likes Alinda. Nyinabarongo said it's because she cut his cord."

"Well then, go and call Tendo from Uncle Kembo's," Father said. "But first bring my foldaway chair."

Father sat in the chair, looking like a chief. The baby had stopped crying, and his eyes were closed. I hoped he would sleep so I could begin preparing the evening meal. We heard the voices of Tendo and Uncle Kembo as they drew closer.

"I was coming to fetch you," Maya said to Tendo, who knitted his brow disapprovingly. Uncle Kembo was limping on his left leg.

"Are you already out of bed?" Father asked him. "How are you feeling now?"

"Still weak and dizzy, but the swelling on my forehead has

come down a bit. It's my leg that's still giving me problems. I hope it wasn't a fracture. How's the baby?"

"He still hasn't drunk any milk, not since yesterday. He cries the whole night, and he is becoming weaker."

"Maybe you need to add some sugar to the milk."

"Sugar? Where on earth would I get sugar? Unless you still know some of those black-market dealers you used to collaborate with."

Uncle Kembo shuffled uncomfortably. "Tendo," he called, "bring me a chair. My leg's hurting."

"So, can you get us some sugar?" Father's voice was unkind.

"I really don't know. I don't have contact with those people anymore. I haven't drunk sugar in my own house for years now, ever since I fell out with . . . with those . . ." Uncle Kembo sounded tired, and he seemed to be pleading with Father to understand.

"Sugar, soap, paraffin, medicine . . . those are things we forgot about long ago, ever since the Indians were chased away, and the factories collapsed, and the rich countries refused to help us. Everyone has been watching and saying nothing as we suffer and drop dead like flies. Unless, of course, you belong to the inner circles of the Muslims, the Army, or the people from West Nile."

Uncle Kembo sighed and passed his right hand across his brow.

"It must be the *ebino*," he said, gazing at the baby. "Have you applied the herbs the Lendu woman gave you?"

"Don't talk to me about that woman in my compound!" Father's mood turned hostile. "She's a witch!" he continued in the same harsh tone. "What I don't understand is why Alinda decided to call her to check the baby when we know so well about her wizard-like ways."

"Hey, don't blame the young girl," Uncle Kembo retorted authoritatively. "Remember, she first called Nyinabarongo when the baby developed diarrhea and a fever. And she was the one who advised Alinda to call the Lendu woman after realizing that *ebino* were bothering the baby, and it was only the Lendu woman who could extract them."

"But how can people be so cruel!" Father's voice was rising in anger. "How can you inflict so much pain on an innocent child? I am sure there were no *ebino* to begin with. The Lendu woman must have planted them in his mouth when she came to check him, so we could pay her money to extract them. How come before she came to our village, babies never used to suffer from *ebino*? We should expel her!"

"You cannot expel her while her husband is not here. You would have to wait for him to come back from Zaire, and that won't be until after the war."

"But if anything happens to my baby, I will not wait for any further reasons to expel her. I will throw her out myself!" Father shouted. "We cannot afford another death in this family," he added after some time, speaking slowly, water forming in his eyes. "We've had enough . . . seen enough . . . God knows we cannot take any more," he shook his head vigorously.

"But you should still apply those herbs she gave you. They helped my boy, remember," Uncle Kembo said in a persuasive tone.

There was silence. I carried the baby inside and placed him on my bed, where he now slept with me. I came back to the yard and found Uncle Kembo and Father still seated in silence. I went to the kitchen to start preparing the evening meal. Tendo had gone to collect the goats from the bush, and Maya was fetching water.

ten

The baby continued to grow more sick. The fluids seeping from his mouth were now a mixture of saliva and pus, and they smelled like milk gone bad. Nyinabarongo came to see us one morning and persuaded Father to let her apply the herbs that the Lendu woman had given us.

"It happened to both of my children," Nyinabarongo told him. "After extracting the *ebino*, you have to apply the herbs to dry the wounds. Otherwise, they will rot and start producing pus. Look at this baby; he is now running a high temperature!"

"I wish I could take him to the hospital so they might give him an injection. I'm sure it would work faster," Father lamented. "And this Lendu woman, she hasn't even come to see the baby! She's a real witch! She should go back to wherever she came from. We don't need foreigners here."

"I saw her on my way over here," Nyinabarongo replied. "She fears to face you because of your bad temper, and she's upset that you are now calling her a witch."

"Well, isn't she? Who bewitched this baby, then? Me?" Father was indignant.

"But when my first child suffered from *ebino* I wasn't even living here. Anyhow, this baby needs help. Let me apply the herbs. You know all the hospitals are closed."

Father fell silent. Nyinabarongo asked me for the herbs the Lendu woman had left with me. I told her they had dried up and would not produce any juice. She said she would go back to the Lendu woman and get fresh ones. Father still did not say anything. When Nyinabarongo returned, she asked me to boil some water, and when it was ready, she mixed it with salt, ginger, and the green herbs she had brought from the Lendu woman. She squeezed them using both hands.

"Come and hold the baby," she told Father, "and open his mouth wide. Alinda, bring a clean piece of cloth."

"Won't it hurt?" Father asked.

"Not as much as it must be hurting now. Look at that pus, and the smell!"

Father looked at me. "Maybe Alinda can hold him. I will go and find Maya and Tendo and tell them to start preparing lunch."

I took the baby and placed his lower body between my thighs, then crossed my legs over his tiny body. He looked too weak to fight. I forced his jaw open by placing my forefinger inside the roof of his mouth and, using my other hand, pressed my thumb on his lower jaw.

The weals had turned yellowish and were covered with a thick coating of pus. Nyinabarongo dropped a little juice on the swollen gums and used the husks of the herbs to press on them. The baby flapped his little hands in the air and tried to turn his head away. "Hold him more tightly," Nyinabarongo commanded me as she continued pressing. She used the clean piece of cloth I had brought to wipe away the pus.

Father came back with Maya. "How is it?" he asked.

Nyinabarongo did not answer immediately. She continued pressing. The baby was now crying loudly and fighting more vigorously. I had problems keeping him still, even though I had thought that he was too weak to fight.

"We have to do this at least three times a day," Nyinabarongo finally answered. "The gums are swollen with pus, and the warm water will burst them and release it. You have to do this again tonight, and you have to force him to drink some milk. He's growing very weak."

After Nyinabarongo had left, the baby stopped crying and slept. I took him to my bed and covered him with a heavy blanket. His body was cooler; his temperature seemed to have gone down. My eyelids were heavy, and my eyes smarting. I wished I could sleep, but I had to wash his nappies.

Maya was seated in the kitchen cutting a pineapple, and she called me to have a slice before I began doing the baby's laundry.

"You should be preparing lunch instead of cutting pineapples. And look, you haven't removed the eyes."

"I tried, but I ended up cutting off all the flesh."

"You should use the tip of the knife. I'm going to do the baby's washing. Is there water in the jerry cans?"

"No," Maya answered. "Tendo was supposed to fetch some, but Father has been looking for him and can't find him. Why don't you take the nappies to the well and wash them there?"

"I can't do that. You can't wash a small baby's nappies at the well!"

"Why?"

"The teeth won't grow."

"But this one has already grown teeth . . . well, they are *ebino*, I suppose . . . killer teeth."

"Yes, those were the killer teeth that grow as a result of witchcraft," I agreed. "Otherwise, this baby is not old enough to grow real teeth—he's not even a month old! And isn't he crying? Is he awake already? Bring him to me."

Maya came back holding the baby. "There was pus on the pillow. It smells!" she said.

The baby started crying more loudly. "Here, hold him. You know he doesn't like the rest of us."

"Warm some milk," I told Maya. "He must be hungry."

When the milk had warmed, I used a teaspoon to pour a little of it into his mouth, but he started crying again.

"Maybe we can give him some pineapple," Maya suggested.

"No, he's too young to eat solid food. You have to help me hold him down so we can force a little more milk into his mouth."

Maya pressed her thumb and forefinger on the baby's cheeks

and forced his mouth open. We fed him some milk, and he slept again.

Father came back with Tendo. "How's the baby?" he asked.

"He's taken some milk," Maya answered. "And you, Tendo, where did you disappear to? There is no water in the jerry cans."

"He went to help Uncle Kembo, whose head is hurting again. Kembo's other leg is swollen as well," Father answered for him.

In the afternoon, the old man came to visit us. We had just finished eating and were seated in the yard. "I'm coming from the Center," he told Father. "People are beginning to return from where they were hiding after the killings. When is this war going to end?"

"I don't know," Father answered. "I hear the Liberators have captured the city. They should now be thinking of coming to rescue us."

"Haven't you heard that they have overrun the Masindi Army Barracks—only forty kilometers from here. They will be here soon. How's the baby?"

"He is much better today—well, at least he has taken some milk."

The old man was carrying a small gourd, oval-shaped like a light bulb, which he said contained goat's milk. "This milk contains natural sugar," he explained. "It's not much, but Alinda can boil it and give some to the baby, especially at nightfall. It will help him to sleep because it also contains a natural sedative." He handed me the calabash, and I thanked him.

"Someone's coming," Maya said, pointing towards the approaching figure. Father made a visor with his right hand and turned his head slightly in the direction of Maya's finger. It was the Lendu woman. She came and sat on the mat with Maya and me. After she had greeted us, she asked about the baby.

"They say he's better today," the old man replied.

"I have brought some sugar," the Lendu woman said.

"Oh!" Father sounded genuinely pleased. "Where did you get it?"

"My husband brought some from Zaire last time he came home, and I saved a little of it."

"Thank you very much," Father said.

The Lendu woman nodded. The old man stood up to leave, and Father said he would accompany him to his house.

After they had left, the Lendu woman turned to me and said, "I don't like the way your father goes on about my being a witch. I only tried to save the baby. If I had not extracted the *ebino*, he would have died."

I started to say something, but she stopped me.

"When Patrice Lumumba was killed by the Americans in 1961, there was a lot of fighting in Zaire. The people staged an uprising in protest, and the Americans sent in troops to put down the demonstrations. I was fifteen at the time, but I had never been to school. I was living with my aunt in Stanleyville, helping her with the children.

"She worked as a nurse at the big hospital, and when the fighting started, she recruited me, together with other young girls, to work as volunteers with her. There were no medicines, so we had to use herbs to treat the soldiers' wounds. That's how I came to learn a lot about different plants, but unfortunately, most of the good ones don't grow here because the climate is harsh, and the soil is not as rich as it is back home.

"When the fighting stopped, I left the hospital and started treating people, using the knowledge I had acquired. Many babies suffering from *ebino* used to be brought to me. The first signs are usually diarrhea and a fever, at times accompanied by vomiting, which might be mistaken for symptoms associated with growing of milk teeth, if the baby is of teeth-growing age. But as I have explained before, these are not really milk teeth . . . some evil people bewitch babies, which causes the tooth buds to rot. If you don't extract the infected tooth bud, the child will die.

"After the operation, you have to apply strong herbs to the wounds; otherwise, the baby can contract an infection and still die.

"But the people in this village have labeled me a witch! I asked for the money only because it is a requirement when you are treating patients with herbs. If you don't attach a monetary value to the treatment, it ceases to be effective. In any case, it's only a token. The people here also say that my husband is a bad man because the fish he sells them is expensive. Yet he goes to a lot of trouble to get that fish from the River Congo, which is very deep and difficult to navigate."

Silence fell upon us. The Lendu woman stood up abruptly and declared that she had to go back to her house. I followed her with my eyes as she walked away. She walked with quick, short steps, the tassels at the bottom of her *kanga* streaming out behind her.

eleven

Uncle Kembo's troubles began when Idi Amin chased the Indians away from Uganda. Before then, he had worked at the Indian-owned sawmill as a night watchman. When the Indians left, the sawmill closed down. He became very poor, and Father started paying school fees for his two children. Whenever there was an important function at our church, his wife would borrow one of Mother's best *gomesi* to wear to the event.

Then the District Leader of the Muslims called Uncle Kembo to his office, and when Uncle Kembo returned to us, he told Mother that he was going to become a Muslim. She sent a message to Father in the city, and he came immediately. There was a bitter argument. Father did not want his brother to become a Muslim, but Uncle Kembo said he had made up his mind and nothing would stop him. Father said that if he converted to Islam, Uncle Kembo would no longer be his brother. It would be a disgrace to the whole family.

A few weeks later, a big party was given in Uncle Kembo's honor at the District Leader's house, but Father refused to go. He said that one could not change from being a Christian to being a Muslim just like that. He suspected that Uncle Kembo had another motive.

But many people attended the party, and Uncle Kembo gave

a speech, telling all the people how pleased he was to have become a Muslim. He was later circumcised, and his name was changed to Abdullah. Then he was given a shop in town, full of free merchandise that had once belonged to an Indian businessman who had been chased away.

Uncle Kembo's wife refused to convert to Islam and continued going to our church with Mother. Uncle Kembo was very cross with her, and he married another woman whom he put in charge of the shop. He stopped coming home to his village and told his two sons, who were Tendo's age and best friends with him, that if they did not convert to Islam he would disown them.

After a few years, he married another woman and said he would soon marry a fourth in order to comply with Islam, which allowed men to marry up to four wives. He came home to his village only during Ramadan—the month of fasting. His first wife told Mother that Uncle Kembo was not able to spend a whole day without eating, but as he did not want his Muslim wives to know this, he expected her to feed him. She always refused to cook for him, however, and so he would come to our house to eat, so long as Father was not there.

Tendo would visit Uncle Kembo secretly at his shop, because he wanted to play with his cousins, who had moved to town to be with their father and stepmothers, and he would return bringing sweets and milk. When Father found out, he forbade Tendo to go there again, so Tendo stopped. During Ramadan, Uncle Kembo would bring us sugar and soap, saying that Ramadan was a period for sharing and giving. Mother would hide these things when Father came to visit us from the city. She said Father was being unreasonable, because we needed to eat, and we could not afford these things.

Uncle Kembo made money from trading on the black market, selling goods that had been illegally imported into the country from Zaire and Kenya. He used his profits to build two more houses for his second and third wives. He also bought two cars, one of which he operated as a special hire service.

He became very generous and allowed his wives' relatives and their friends to take goods on credit, but they never paid him back. Eventually, the stock dried up, and he did not have enough money to replace it, so the shop collapsed. His two Muslim wives left him. He sold the cars and came back to live with his first wife in the village. He said he had become a Christian again and even started going to church. He and Father were reconciled.

The day we buried Kaaka, Uncle Kembo almost died. He was standing near the grave, holding a spade, ready to shovel in some soil, when he suddenly started shaking and fell into the grave. When he was rescued, he was still shaking, and there was foam at the corners of his mouth. Father said it was the curse of Kaaka. When Uncle Kembo had converted to Islam, she had cursed him and told him never to go near her grave when she died. Now he was walking with a limp, and his forehead was still swollen after the fall.

The day we buried Kaaka, there were three graves. The smallest was for the baby that was said to have been discovered in Kaaka's stomach. It was wrapped in bark-cloth, and I could not get a glimpse of it.

The third grave was Mother's.

There were only a few people at the burial, because they were too scared to come out of their houses for fear of meeting the soldiers, who continued to roam around the village. The day they shot Kaaka, they also killed two other villagers, whom they had met at the Center, coming from a church meeting.

Father tried to make a speech at the burial but ended up crying so hard that the old man had to assist him back to the house. Maya was hysterical and attempted to throw herself into Mother's grave, but she was restrained by the Lendu woman, who seemed to be the only strong one. Tendo looked grave and calm, but his eyes were hot red. Afterwards, I sat on the red soil that had been scooped out of the graves, my head reeling and feeling dizzy. A river of tears streamed down my face, and I had neither the will nor the strength to stop them. What would life be like without Mother? Without Kaaka? And what was going to happen to the baby? Would we survive this war?

No official mourning ceremonies were carried out, but an air of mourning and a sense of emptiness and despair hung over us. We never went back to sleep in the bushes again, and Nyinabarongo spent three days at our house, showing me how to mind the baby and telling me again and again that I had to be strong.

"Was that a real baby that was discovered in Kaaka's stomach?" I asked Nyinabarongo one day.

"Yes, it was," she answered.

"But how could it have lived there for so long? I mean, Kaaka was about 60 or 70."

"It was a child of the spirits."

"What does that mean? A child of the spirits?"

"It's a long story." Nyinabarongo said. "When Kaaka was a young girl, she came across two snakes making love in the fields where she had gone to collect food. She placed her *kanga* close to where they were rolling, intertwined, and soon it was wrapped round their bodies. This way, the fluids from their mating gave the *kanga* permanent medicinal value.

"She rushed home to tell her mother, thrilled that she would now be able to cure people of snakebites, using the water washed from the *kanga*. But her mother was not excited.

"'My daughter,' her mother told her. 'This means you will never get married! People like you, who possess such medicine, belong to the community. They can never leave. It would have been fine were you a boy, because then you would marry and remain here in your community. But as a girl, you have to go away when you get married, and you cannot transfer your luck to anyone else!'

"'But I want to get married, Mother,' Kaaka begged. 'I am already in love!'

"'That cannot be.'

"'But I am already pregnant, Mother. I was just going to tell you. My man wants to marry me immediately!'

"'You have shamed me, my daughter. We will have to visit a

strong medicine man who will make the pregnancy invisible, so that when you do marry, no one will suspect that you were already pregnant.'

"After about a year of marriage, Kaaka came back to tell her mother that she had failed to deliver the baby and that her stomach was still swollen. They went back to the medicine man, but unfortunately, he had long since died. Kaaka's stomach remained swollen since that time. They say she used to beat her husband mercilessly whenever he accused her of having failed to deliver their baby. Eventually, she left him and came to live with your father."

twelve

Jungu came to see me when she heard about the death of my mother. Father exclaimed at how tall and mature she had grown in the few months since he had last seen her.

"Goodness! You now look like a fully-grown woman! But aren't you Alinda's age?"

"Yes, we were born in the same year." Jungu answered shyly. "We both turned thirteen this July."

"But tell me, aren't the fleeing soldiers bothering you as much as they are us? Have they killed anyone in your village?"

"No, but maybe it's because we are not as close to the main road as you are. We only hear gunshots at night when they are terrorizing people in the Center."

"But which route did you take to reach us? Weren't you afraid that you would meet the soldiers on your way?"

"I was, but my brother escorted me, and we used the footpaths."

"Perhaps we should consider moving to your village," Father said thoughtfully, turning to look at me. "I could build a small thatched hut, and we could stay there until this war is over. This village is becoming increasingly dangerous! And the Liberators are nowhere to be seen! We used to hide in the banana plantation at night, but since the death . . . since the killings . . . and the baby. . . ." His voice trailed off, and he blinked back the tears in his eyes. I felt like crying too and comforting Father at the same time. He looked so vulnerable!

Jungu looked at us anxiously and said quietly, "I'm sure my grandmother wouldn't mind lending you a piece of land. You should talk to her."

Nyinabarongo had become a regular visitor. Every day, she would come to check on the baby's progress, and then stay on and eat meals with us. I saw her approaching now, a *kanga* thrown lightly around her shoulders.

"Where did you leave your child?" Maya asked her.

"Sleeping."

"Alone?"

"Yes. I locked the door. I won't stay long this time."

"Why? We're cooking lunch!" I protested.

We were still seated in the kitchen where we had eaten our breakfast. A light drizzle was falling, a reminder of last night's heavy storm. Jungu was wearing my sweater, the sleeves of which stopped some inches above her wrists. I had wrapped Mother's long dress around my shoulders. Maya was playing with the baby on the mat.

"I passed by my pit to check on the things I'd hidden in it," Nyinabarongo said. "I was worried that the rain might have soaked them through."

"Didn't you place an iron sheet over everything before covering the pit with soil?" Maya asked.

"No. I didn't have one to spare. But maybe I shouldn't have worried so much about the rain. The termites have eaten almost my whole blanket and made holes in my mattress!"

"Oh dear!" Jungu exclaimed. "My mother hid our radio in a pit, and I hid my books and school uniform in there too! What will happen if they're eaten by termites?"

"I don't think you should be worrying about school right now," Nyinabarongo said, shaking her head. "What we should be worried about is whether we will survive this war! I don't sleep a wink at night since your father refused to allow us to sleep in the banana grove. I keep imagining the soldiers will come one night and kill me and my child!"

"Alinda, did you hide your books?" Jungu turned to me. "Do you think we'll ever go back to school?"

"I have to think of the baby first," I answered. "Who'll take care of him if I go back to school?"

"I'm sure he'd be fine," Nyinabarongo answered. "There are many children who grow up without their mothers."

"And how's your first child, the one you left with his father?" Maya asked.

"Why did you leave him behind?" Jungu added before Nyinabarongo could reply.

"His father said I could only take the girl."

"Because she was younger?" Jungu pressed her.

"No, I don't think so. Even if the boy had been younger, his father would still have insisted that I take the girl. He believes boys are more important than girls. I should never have married that man!"

"Did they force you?" Jungu's tone was gentle.

"No—well—I mean not really. But I didn't have a choice. You see, my father died when my sisters and I were still young; actually, I was the youngest. The teachers said I was very clever. I would always come first in my class. My mother wanted to keep me in school, so she decided to marry off our eldest sister and use the money from her bride-price to pay for my school fees.

"My sister had been married only for a year when she suddenly died. We never got to know what really happened. Her husband then demanded that he be paid back some of the bride-price. My mother had already used part of it to repair our house and the rest to pay my school fees. My sister's husband said that if my mother could not pay back the money, he would take one of us as his wife. I was about fourteen then."

A shadow darkened the doorway. I looked up to see Father standing there and Tendo lingering behind him. He greeted Nyinabarongo and told her that he had been to see Uncle Kembo.

"How is he?" she asked him.

"He's getting worse. He can hardly walk. Both his legs are

now horribly swollen, and he has a terrible headache from the blow to his head. We've been slashing the weeds in his compound—actually, all the footpaths need clearing if one of us isn't going to step on a snake!"

"And the well needs cleaning as well," Nyinabarongo added. "The undergrowth has crept right into the water."

"It's the war," Father sounded resigned, "None of us has the will to keep our yards clean when we don't know if we will survive!"

It was just at that moment that we heard the explosion. The walls of the kitchen shook, and the ground trembled as if an earthquake were shaking us. Maya screamed. Jungu fell to the ground and curled herself into a ball. Nyinabarongo shouted, "My child!" and ran off to find her. Tendo ducked for the window, hoisted himself through it, and fell outside. Father said in a shaky voice, "What on earth was that?"

I was still seated on the mat. I tried to lift my legs, but they felt as heavy as pieces of wet wood.

A shrill cry of "Help! Please help!" pierced the air.

"Someone's been hurt," Father said and started moving in the direction of the cry. I tried to stand up but failed. Fear seemed to have seeped into my legs, making them numb. The baby was crying.

Father was calling for people to help him. Jungu raised her head, and I motioned her to pick up the baby. Her eyes were watering from the dust from the blast.

"What was that?" she whispered. "Where is everybody?"

Maya and Tendo had heeded Father's call.

"Please pick up the baby," I said to Jungu. "I'm scared! Something has happened to my legs." She lifted the child from the mat and hushed him soothingly. I rubbed my legs until they began to tingle, then slowly stood up.

We walked to the scene of the explosion. The old man was lying in the shrubs, a few meters away from the footpath that led from his house to ours. The grass was crimson with his blood, and his right leg was dangling by a fragile piece of skin at the knee. Words were bubbling from his mouth.

"It was a landmine!" Father's voice was just a whisper, his face ashen. "Who could have planted it on a footpath?" He was holding a small, shell-shaped metallic object, tentatively turning it around in his hands, as if it might explode again.

Uncle Kembo was approaching, leaning his tall frame on the shoulders of the Lendu woman. "What's this?" he asked, looking dazed. Nyinabarongo had already arrived, her child securely tied to her back. We all stood there, transfixed.

The Lendu woman broke the spell. She drew nearer and examined the old man's shattered leg. It did not look like a leg at all! From the knee downwards, it was just a mass of red meat from which small pieces of white bone protruded. The toes had been severed.

"We have to remove it," the Lendu woman said, gingerly touching it with the tips of her fingers. "We will use a saw," she added grimly.

"A saw?" Father and Uncle Kembo echoed in disbelief.

"Yes. We will need a very sharp one. The bone is already shattered. What is holding the knee to the thigh is only the muscles, which can be severed easily with a saw."

"I only have a panga," Uncle Kembo's voice was trembling. "It's the one I used when I was still working as a night watchman. It's very sharp."

"No," the Lendu woman protested. "A panga's edge is thick and blunt. We need a small, thin saw."

"What about the one Father has been using to kill the goats?" Maya offered.

"Yes," Father chipped in. He was still standing a short distance away from us, his face averted. "Tendo, go and fetch it. It's hanging in a sheath behind the kitchen door."

Tendo snapped to attention when he heard his name. He had backed off when the Lendu woman had started talking of amputating the old man's leg. Jungu nudged closer to me and whispered in my ear, "Are they going to cut off the leg?"

I nodded. A lump seemed to have grown in my throat, and when I swallowed, it bobbed up and down like an Adam's apple.

The old man sat up abruptly, supporting himself on his

elbows. "Please . . ." he struggled to speak. His voice was faint. "Don't cut off my leg. I came into this world whole, I want to leave it whole."

"We have to do this," the Lendu woman said urgently. "And we have to stop this bleeding; otherwise, he will go into shock. Has Tendo brought the saw?" Tendo had not moved.

"Can someone please bring the saw!" the Lendu woman was now shouting. She unwound her *kanga* from her waist and started folding it. Jungu passed the baby to me and said she was going to fetch the saw. Uncle Kembo went and sat on a tree trunk, holding his head in his hands. The Lendu woman called Nyinabarongo to assist her as she tied her *kanga* tightly around the mutilated leg.

Jungu came back with the saw.

"You have to hold him down," the Lendu woman said, addressing Nyinabarongo and Jungu. "The numbness will have worn off by now. We should have done this immediately."

Maya stepped forward. "I can also help," she said bravely.

"Get a piece of cloth and cover his eyes," the Lendu woman told her. "If he doesn't see what we're doing, he won't feel the pain as much."

Maya rushed over to me and grabbed the piece of cloth that was covering the baby. "But this is for the baby," I protested.

Maya did not respond. She ran back and placed the cloth gently over the old man's eyes. All the fight seemed to have gone out of him. He did not protest.

Everyone seemed to be talking at once. Tendo had retreated and was standing on an anthill. Father was holding Nyinabarongo's child, shaking his head in disbelief.

"Jungu, you will hold down his good leg, and Nyinabarongo will take care of the arms," the Lendu woman said, examining the small saw in her hands. She seemed satisfied.

Still holding the baby tightly in my arms, I started walking away, placing one foot in front of the other, slowly at first, then more quickly, until I had put a distance between my weary body and the scene of blood. As I continued walking, I could still hear faint sounds of their conversation rising through the air.

part three

thirteen

Faint sounds continued to stream into the bedroom where I lay. I opened my eyes, seeing the sun filtering through the cracks in the shutters and coming under the door.

I felt more than saw someone entering the bedroom. Turning my head slightly, I realized it was Jungu, and she was carrying a basin. She came and sat on a small stool near the foot of my bed. She retrieved a tin of Vaseline from the open suitcase on the table in the corner and started smearing her body with the jelly. She slipped her *kangu* from her shoulders, and it fell softly on the floor. She creamed Vaseline around her collarbone and down towards her breasts. From her suitcase, she retrieved a comb and pulled it through her wavy, wet hair. Little particles of water sparkled and scattered over my forehead, and I blinked my eyes.

I could now feel her moving silently as a shadow towards the rack where we kept our clothes. After she had dressed, she pushed the basin under my bed and moved out of the room.

When I opened my eyes again, both windows were open. The smell of freshly cut grass filled my nostrils. I turned my head briefly and looked through the window, trying to place the sounds I could hear outside. There seemed to be many people speaking in chorus, responding to statements barked gruffly by their leader. Their voices rose and fell, like waves, until they drifted away into the distance, and I slept again.

The next time I woke up, Jungu was sitting on the edge of my bed, gingerly touching a part of my arm that was not covered by blankets.

"You're awake at last!" she said.

I tried to speak, but my lips seemed to be stuck together, and my tongue felt heavy in my mouth. Father was standing in the doorway.

"How are you feeling, Alinda?" he asked, worriedly. "It's good to see you awake."

Ringing tones buzzed in my ears. I closed my eyes.

When I woke again, it was late afternoon. Beads of cold sweat had formed on my neck, and when I moved my head, they trickled in slow motion down to the space between my breasts. I struggled out of bed, and a wave of nausea and dizziness hit me. I leaned on the doorframe and vomited. Jungu came rushing in.

"You're vomiting! My God, but you haven't eaten anything since yesterday. Lie down again. Would you like some tea?"

I wanted to ask her to bring me water to rinse my mouth, but I didn't want to speak for fear I would swallow the particles of food still in my mouth. Father was standing by the window, watching us anxiously. Jungu started leading me towards the bed. But I wanted to rinse my mouth! I would have to risk speaking.

"It must have been the meat," I said, the sound of my voice surprising me.

"Meat? But you haven't eaten meat in a long time now!" Father said.

"It reminds me of blood—Mother's afterbirth, and the old man's leg," the words forced themselves out of my dry lips. "How's the baby? And where's Tendo?" I added before they could respond. I wanted to stop talking because my voice sounded strange, and it frightened me.

I folded my lips and passed my tongue over them, tasting blood. Now I wanted to laugh because I thought my lips must look funny, folded in like that. I heard a loud echo of laughter rumbling in the pit of my stomach.

Father moved from the window, and I heard him tell Jungu to leave me to rest.

fourteen

Two weeks later, I was still bedridden. The Liberators had arrived. I was eager to see them but was told that they lived near the forest on the large expanse of land that belonged to Uncle Kembo.

Nyinabarongo had taken over the running of our house during the time I was sick and the days that followed my recovery. Jungu minded the baby, and Maya took charge of the lighter chores.

One afternoon, when I was beginning to feel strong enough to go outside, Nyinabarongo came and joined me under the mango tree. She said I needed to exercise a little since I had lain in bed for so long. She asked me to accompany her to the old man's house since she was going to check on his health.

We found the old man lying on a mat in the shade of a small avocado tree. Thick shrubs and tall guava trees surrounded the house, which was small and roofed with rusted corrugated iron sheets.

I inched forward hesitantly, not knowing how he would receive me, or whether Mother's ghost would be angry with me, since she had forbidden us to ever visit him. I had never been there before. Nyinabarongo found a short wooden bench inside the house that she carried outside, and she beckoned me to sit on it with her. The old man did not seem to know that we were there. His eyes roamed aimlessly around the yard, and he constantly licked his dry lips.

Nyinabarongo got up and knelt by his side, feeling his forehead. I avoided looking at the stump, which looked freshly bandaged with a *kanga*, and instead concentrated on the old man's remaining foot, noticing that the big toe pointed away from the rest of the toes, which made it look rather strange.

"Are you still in pain?" Nyinabarongo asked gently.

"Yes," he groaned, trying to turn his head, "especially my toes. That's where the greatest pain is." Droplets of sweat were streaming down his face.

"He's running a very high temperature," Nyinabarongo said. "I think you'd better fetch the Lendu woman and ask her to bring some of her herbs."

I walked off quickly, almost running, feeling pleased with myself that I was finally regaining my strength. I stopped to pick some guava fruits, which were lying under the trees, and stuffed them in the pockets of my dress. The Lendu woman was not at her house, and I proceeded to Uncle Kembo's to ask him if he knew where she was. I found her there, washing Uncle Kembo's clothes. They both commented on how much better I looked. I had to wait for the Lendu woman as she went to collect the herbs that grew in her compound.

"He says the pain is mainly in his toes, even though the toes are not there," I told the Lendu woman as we walked to the old man's house.

"It's only in his mind," she replied. "He must have stepped on the landmine with those toes."

"Will the wound heal?"

"Yes, but it will take a long time. He's an old man, and the tissues cannot be expected to grow back easily. He has to eat well, and besides, he has lost a lot of blood. The wound needs to be cleaned and dressed at least twice a day. These are strong herbs," she added, holding out the green, thin leaves wound around thorny branches for me to see. "They cause a burning sensation that can be unbearable at times, but that wound needs strong medicine."

We reached the old man's house, and she started to boil the herbs. She said she would stay with him until his temperature subsided.

"It's some kind of punishment from God," Nyinabarongo said as we walked towards our house.

"Why do you say that?" I asked, surprised.

"You don't know his story?"

"No."

"Your mother never told you?"

"No, she only used to say that he was a dangerous man and we should never go near his house."

"She was right. That man! He came to live in our village about six years ago, soon after he had been released from prison. When Idi Amin came to power in 1971, he wanted to convert all the people to Islam. Some were persuaded by a lot of money, like your uncle. Then the prisoners who were serving life sentences were told that if they converted to Islam, the president would pardon them. The old man fell into that category."

"But why was he in prison anyway? He looks so harmless!"

"He murdered his wife!" Nyinabarongo answered bluntly. "They say he used to love meat so much, that one evening, he bought a lot of it and took it home to his wife to roast. He told her he was going to town with his friends to buy drinks, and when they returned, they should find it ready, so they could wash it down with the alcohol. It was two days before Christmas, and everyone was in a festive mood.

"His wife did as she was told. But they didn't come back. She waited the whole night, and the whole of the following day, but they did not return.

"His wife disliked meat, so she would not eat it, and even if she'd wanted to, there was too much of it. So she decided to take it to her parents, whose house was close by. Her husband returned, dead drunk, when she was still with her parents. And by the time she returned, he had worked himself into a murderous frenzy. He asked for his meat, and she told him she'd just given it to her parents. 'Go and get it back,' he demanded. She said she couldn't do that, as it would be very improper. 'So your parents love meat, eh!' he said. That's when he got a panga and started cutting her into pieces. When he finished, he put the pieces into a gunnysack, tied it on his bicycle, and rode to her parents' home. 'I have brought you more meat. I understand you love it very much.'

"By the time they discovered that it was their daughter in the gunnysack, the man was long gone. They raised an alarm, and the villagers joined in the search. They found him about to hang himself from a tree near the well. He refused to descend, and they had to cut the tree down.

"The villagers were so angry that they fell on him and beat him. They even pulled out his teeth so that he would never be able to eat meat again. After Amin released him, he feared to go back to his village. Your uncle gave him a piece of land here because at that time he had also just converted to Islam."

"But Mother used to tell us that the old man had given land to the Lendu people."

"Well . . . yes, but he did not *give* it to them, he *sold* it to them. They say he was released from prison with some money and a sewing machine, to enable him to start a new life.

"He later sold the sewing machine on credit to your uncle, who hired it out to a woman who sewed from the verandah outside his shop.

"When Uncle Kembo lost his money, and later the shop, he failed to pay the old man for the sewing machine. So the old man demanded that he give him a piece of land as payment. That's how he came to sell part of it to the Lendu people, who had run away from their own homeland because of the war there.

"Now God is punishing him. He will die a terrible death, just like his wife," Nyinabarongo concluded.

"How long did he spend in prison?"

"Sixteen years."

"Did they have any children?"

"No. Their marriage was still young."

We reached the house, and I gave some of the guavas to Nyinabarongo's child, who was playing with Maya. Father was splitting firewood, and Jungu was washing the dishes with the baby strapped to her back. When the baby saw me, he struggled to come to me, and I undid the cloth from Jungu and took him in my arms.

"Alinda, it's good to see you looking well today. Where have you two been?" Father asked.

"We've been to see the old man," Nyinabarongo answered.

"Is he better?"

"No, but the Lendu woman is trying to bring down his temperature."

Father continued splitting the firewood, placing his right foot firmly at the base of the log to prevent it from rolling, then bringing down the axe on it. A small splinter jumped and landed on Nyinabarongo's child's forehead. She screamed and ran to her mother.

"That's enough," Nyinabarongo said. "There is more in the kitchen."

Father wiped his brow with the tip of his sleeve. "You're sure it will take us through tomorrow?"

But Nyinabarongo did not hear. She was already on her way to the kitchen, carrying some of the firewood in her arms, like a baby.

"Where have you been all day?" I asked Maya and Jungu. "I was looking for you this afternoon.

"We went to visit our friends."

"Which friends?"

"The Liberators," said Maya. "Ask Jungu to take you there; she has a good friend among them."

I turned to Jungu questioningly.

"I will take you . . . tomorrow," she answered, a smile growing wide on her face.

"You missed the party we had for them at Uncle Kembo's house when they first arrived," Maya said. "Father slaughtered the two remaining goats, and Uncle Kembo brought a third. There was so much meat!"

"They roasted all three goats over a big fire, and we ate so well, we finished it all," Jungu added.

"Nyinabarongo brought four chickens, and we couldn't find enough saucepans to cook them in. I was sent to fetch those we had hidden in the pit, but by the time I came back, the Liberators had become impatient and were already cooking the chickens in their helmets!" Maya laughed, and we laughed with her.

"The Lendu woman asked them to go and liberate Zaire too, after they were finished with Uganda, and kill or chase away that dictator, Mobutu," Jungu said.

"What did they say?" I asked.

"Their commander said it was not possible because it was wrong for one country to attack another."

"Father went to the Center and bought some beer and invited more people to come and celebrate with us. We ate and danced the whole night!" Maya's excitement was still clearly visible.

I could not believe that I had missed all that.

The following morning I woke up feeling even stronger. I saw Tendo for the first time since I had fallen sick. He was washing his face, which was covered with soapsuds. I greeted him, and he replied with his eyes closed.

"I've not seen you in a while," I said to him.

"Hey, you were sick all the time. I came to your room, but you didn't even recognize me."

"That's not what I mean."

"You mean since yesterday?"

"Yes. Father was splitting firewood because you were nowhere to be seen."

"I was with my friend, Mwiso. He's young like me, you know. He dropped out of school to train in the army."

"But you should be helping with some housework."

"Uncle Kembo gave them a piece of land, the one near the forest to construct their shelters," Tendo continued excitedly. "And they gave him medicine for the swelling on his forehead. It's now come down, and his leg no longer hurts. He's completely cured! The Liberators have such strong medicines!"

"How come they haven't cured the old man's wound? We

went to see him yesterday, and he was still in a lot of pain."

"Well, he has to ask them. How would they know about his wound?"

"You could tell them."

"I will. Now I have to go. I arranged to meet Mwiso after their morning parade. We're going to hunt for porcupines."

Jungu came over to join us. "I want to take you to see the Liberators," she said.

"How many of them are there?"

"There are about two hundred camping on that piece of land Uncle Kembo gave them, but there are many others, perhaps six thousand, who live in town."

"But why are they staying in our village?"

"I don't know. When they first arrived, they stayed here, in your compound, for a few days, but your father complained to their commander that they were harassing Maya and me. At first, their commander didn't believe it. He kept saying that his men were well trained and wouldn't do the things your father was accusing them of."

"What things?"

"Well, it's a long story. I tried to explain to your father that this soldier was just my friend, and that his other friend was interested in making Maya his friend. Anyway, your father became very angry and chased them away. We always pretend that we're going to visit the Lendu woman, as your father would be very upset if he learned that we were visiting the Liberators."

"But we should at least tell Nyinabarongo where we're going; otherwise she'll wonder where we are, and aren't we supposed to help her with the housework? Where does she sleep, by the way?"

"In your father's bedroom. I think they're still asleep. Let's go! I'll fetch the baby."

fifteen

Jungu carried the baby as we walked towards the forest.

"They used to come on their morning parade to our compound until your father complained to their commander that they were making a lot of noise and that you were very ill and needed to rest," Jungu said, referring to the Liberators.

Their shelters were spread across the whole of Uncle Kembo's land, extending to the shrubs near the well, with some spilling over onto our and the Lendu woman's banana plantations. They were thatched with spear grass, and between the big corner poles more grass was tied to smaller poles.

More shelters were visible beyond the thick shrubs where we used to hide from Amin's soldiers during the night. Most of them were empty, and Jungu explained that, at this time of the day, the soldiers were usually either hunting in the fields for squirrels and rabbits or in the village begging for food and money from the villagers.

Biscuit packets and empty meat cans lay everywhere. Some of the open space was taken up by the soldiers' uniforms, which they had washed and spread on the grass to dry. Cold fireplaces took up the rest of the grass together with dirty, soot-covered saucepans and colored plastic cups. Jungu seemed to know her way around, as she dodged through the maze of these assorted items. I followed closely behind. Some of the soldiers shouted greetings at us, above the loud sound from their small radios.

"*Mambo Cheupe.*"—Greetings the white one, one soldier shouted as we passed by his shelter.

"*Poa!*"—Fine! Jungu answered.

"*Huyo ni nani? Sijawahi kumwona.*"—Who's that? I've never seen her before.

"*Huyo ni rafiki yangu.*"—She's my friend.

"*Ni mrembo kweli! Yaani, ningipenda kwenda naye Tanzania.*"—She is really beautiful! I would like to take her back to Tanzania.

Jungu laughed. "Let's go and find Bahati," she said to me.

"How did you learn their language so fast?" I asked her in amazement.

"Kiswahili? I know only a few words, but it's not too difficult. Most of the words are derived from Bantu languages and are similar to our own. Besides, Bahati is keen for me to learn it, so he teaches me. I also teach him English and our language. He told me that he was friends with a Ugandan soldier who has been fighting with him in this war. This soldier is from our area, and he has been teaching him a little of our language."

"I still don't understand why he doesn't speak English. I thought he went to school before he joined the army."

"Yes, he did, but, you see, everyone in Tanzania speaks Kiswahili. It is used in offices, schools, and even among the village people who never went to school. English is only taught in private primary schools as a language of instruction. But in the government ones where the majority go, they use and teach Kiswahili only."

"But what about their own languages? I mean, the languages of their tribes?"

"They don't speak them."

"Then how can they tell what tribe someone belongs to?"

"I'm sure it must be difficult since everyone speaks the same language. Maybe they can tell by their names, you know, just like here; people from different regions have different names."

"I guess I like it better here, where people are able to speak the language of their tribes."

We found Bahati sitting outside his shelter, his head bent between his legs, reading a magazine full of colored pictures. When he heard us coming, he looked up and smiled broadly at Jungu, at the same time folding the magazine and pushing it quickly into his pocket. He had a shy, boyish, round face, but his eyes were sharp and roving.

"*Mtoto hajambo?*"—Is the baby fine? he asked Jungu.

"*Hajambo.*"—He's fine, Jungu answered. "Can we sit down?" she asked him in English.

Bahati smiled and moved to make space for us to sit on the grass with him. The magazine he had been reading popped partially out of his pocket, and Jungu tried to pull it all the way out, but he placed his hand firmly over it. Jungu looked up at him.

"What are you trying to hide from me?" she asked him, again in English.

He kept silent and moved a little further from us. The baby stretched out his hands, wanting to reach him. Bahati turned and moved closer, and the baby fell into his arms. He started bouncing him on his lap. The baby gurgled happily. Bahati turned and looked at me for a brief moment.

"*Jamani! Huyu ndiye alikuwa mgonjwa?*"—Is this the one who has been sick?

Jungu nodded. She seemed annoyed that Bahati had prevented her from looking at the magazine. There followed an awkward silence, the only noise being the baby's gurgles.

I was about to suggest to Jungu that we go back home when we saw Tendo and his friend arriving. Tendo was carrying a dead porcupine dripping with blood. He flung it on the ground near me, and I squirmed and tried to turn away.

"It's dead!" Tendo said with laughter in his voice.

"Take it away, I don't want to see blood."

Bahati looked at me sideways and laughed slowly, covering his mouth with his right hand.

"We're going to cook it for dinner. Won't you eat?" Tendo was still taunting me. He turned to his friend and indicated with various signs that he should bring a knife to cut up the dead animal.

"By the way, this is Mwiso, my friend. I've been trying to

teach him our language, but he has failed to learn it. I've also failed to learn Kiswahili, so we communicate using signs."

Mwiso was a thin boy who stood tall and straight as a reed. He had a hard, unsmiling face, and his small eyes swept over us briefly before he marched off to find the knife.

"How did you kill it?" Jungu asked, staring at the porcupine.

"We smoked it out of its burrow."

"Is that where they live?"

"Yes. They dig deep holes. If you want to kill one, you have to light a fire at the mouth of the burrow so the heat can suffocate it, and it is forced to run. You have to be waiting for it at the exit of the burrow with a sharp, long spear," Tendo laughed.

"And what are those sharp things covering its body?"

"Those are its protective needles. When you attack it, it expands its body and they shoot off, like arrows. If you are unlucky, they can land right in your eye," Tendo demonstrated using his hands, as if aiming for a bird with a bow and arrow, his left eye tightly closed.

Bahati and Jungu laughed loudly.

"You've never seen a porcupine before?" I asked Jungu.

"No. I guess it's because I live in town."

"It's very tasty. They say it is the fattiest animal in the world," Tendo said.

"In the whole world! I don't believe you."

"Wait till you taste it tonight!"

"Will it be enough for us?" Jungu asked, looking at Bahati.

"Yes. It may look small, but it weighs about fifteen kilograms."

"But how does it support all that weight on those short legs?"

"They are short but very strong. It's the feet that are tender and smooth, see, just like a baby's."

When Mwiso brought the knife, I stood up and told Jungu that I was going back home.

"Wait a bit please," she said to me.

I shook my head, nausea already washing over me. I began walking away, and when I looked back, Jungu had not moved. I leaned on a tree and waited for her.

"Are you all right?" she asked when she caught up with me.

"Yes."

"Then let's go."

At home, Nyinabarongo had already prepared lunch. She looked at me and asked if I was feeling all right, and I said that I needed to go and lie down for a bit. I felt nauseated.

When I opened my eyes, it was already dark, and the baby was crying in the next room where he now slept with Maya. Maya said he was hungry and asked me to carry him as she went to the kitchen to warm his milk. I felt too tired even to stand up, and I told her so.

"Why don't you ask Jungu?"

"She's not here," Maya said.

"Where does she go at this time of the night?" I asked.

"It's not yet eight, and she must be with her boyfriend."

"And where are Father and Nyinabarongo?"

"They said they were going for a walk."

Jungu came back while Maya was still in the kitchen.

"I've brought you some biscuits," she said, handing me two pieces.

I bit into one tentatively. It was tasteless.

"Bahati gave them to me. The soldiers are supplied with them every day."

"It has no taste. What's it made from?" I asked.

"Cassava flour. It fills the stomach so you don't feel hungry quickly. When you eat one for breakfast, you can spend the whole day without feeling like eating again. He has also given me a present," Jungu added, holding out a plastic bag for me to see.

"What is it?" I asked.

"I don't know, I will open it tomorrow so we can look at it properly in daylight."

"Tell me about Bahati," I said. "Do you love him?"

"He's a very nice person. He's genuine and sincere, and

above all, dependable. He's an orphan, and before he joined the army, he used to live with his uncle who didn't treat him well." She paused for a moment.

"He wants to be loved, and often asks me to hold him. He also longs for a family of his own. He loves children very much. And yes, I love him. I want to go with him when they leave. I want to live with him in Tanzania, and I can also become a soldier!"

"Are there women soldiers among them? I've not seen any."

"No, he said their commanders think women are unfit both physically and mentally for fighting. But I can be the first!"

"Have you told your mother about all this?"

"No, because I know she won't approve, but I'm going to tell your father."

We were quiet for some time.

"When we have our baby, Bahati says we'll name her Amani."

"Are you going to have a baby?"

"Yes. I mean at some point, yes, I'd love to have a baby with Bahati. And Alinda, I want my baby to have a father, to know its father. That's why I'm so determined to go with Bahati when they leave," Jungu's voice was fierce.

"He's been giving me presents. Look at this." She retrieved a small object from under her pillow. It was a wristwatch with a metal strap; its silvery color sparkled in the yellow light from the lantern.

"Where did he get it?"

"He told me there was a lot of looting in Kampala when they were chasing away Amin's soldiers. One of his friends found it in a shop. Bahati bought it from him so he could give it to me."

"And what's that you haven't shown me? Another present?"

"Oh! This, no, this is a magazine. Remember the one he was reading this morning when we went to visit him? He said he feared to show it to me when you were around because he doesn't know you well."

"What kind of magazine is it?"

"It has pictures of naked women. It's embarrassing to look at!"

"But where did he get such a magazine?"

"He said he found it in Amin's bedroom in State House! Can you imagine! He went into the president's house and said that there were many such magazines in his bedroom, as well as weapons."

"Is it true that Amin used to keep the heads of his enemies in a refrigerator?"

"I don't know. Bahati never talked of having seen them."

"I'm glad they got rid of that monster! I wonder what happened to him. Do you think he was captured or killed?"

"He escaped! Bahati said he ran to Libya, but their commander believes he's still hiding in his hometown, Arua. He says after they leave here, they are going there to try to capture him, and that it's going to be the biggest battle so far because all of Amin's supporters are hiding there."

"Has the whole country been liberated?"

"Yes, except the area where they suspect Amin is hiding."

"But if they go to Arua and leave us alone here, won't those bad soldiers come back to terrorize us? You know, like those who killed Kaaka?"

"Bahati said most of them drowned in Lake Albert as they were trying to cross into Zaire."

"Well, I really hope we'll be safe."

"I'm sure you will."

"How about you?"

"I've already told you my plan. I am going with them when they leave. No one's going to stop me."

sixteen

In the morning, Jungu came to wake me at nine o'clock. I was still feeling tired from the previous day's attack of nausea.

"Come outside," she said urgently. "Come! Bahati is here to visit us. Father and the others have gone to visit Uncle Kembo, and I want to open the present I showed you last night."

Bahati was seated on the low stool Father always used while eating, a shy smile on his face.

"You can talk to him in English," Jungu said. "He has learned quite a lot, but he feels shy to speak it when there are many people around. I've assured him that you are also his friend and will not laugh at him when he makes mistakes."

"Good morning," I said to him.

"How are you?" he asked.

"Look!" Jungu exclaimed, removing a piece of cotton cloth from the plastic bag she had shown me last evening. She started spreading it out, and asked Bahati to hold two of the corners, while she held the other two. It was rectangular, about two meters long.

"It's a *kanga*!" she said excitedly. "Isn't it beautiful, Alinda!"

I nodded. I had never seen such beautiful colors and designs before. The background was a rich, deep orange, like the color of a sunset, and on it were printed three large flowers, with bursting green and yellow petals. The biggest flower rested in the center, while the two smaller ones stretched out towards the edges. The four borders were each crossed with the same pattern of zigzag black lines, and unlike the locally made *kangas*, this one did not have tassels.

I moved closer to read the inscriptions written in the white-and-black zigzag lines. "*Macho Yameonana Mioyo Ikasemezana,*" Bahati read them out aloud.

"What does it mean?" Jungu and I asked in unison.

"Our eyes met and our hearts began to speak."

Jungu giggled shyly. "Can I make an outfit out of it?"

"Sure," Bahati answered promptly. "An outfit with these colors would look beautiful on you. And this material," he added, feeling the fabric, "is cool and comfortable for our kind of climate. You can wear it any time."

"Where did you get it?" I asked him.

"I bought it in Tanzania. There are many factories that make them. I just thought–that–well, that I might meet a . . . a . . . *rafiki* . . . a friend," he spoke haltingly, searching for the correct English word to substitute for the Kiswahili one. He looked at us shyly, uncomfortably.

"Teach me a little of Kiswahili," I said to him after a time.

"What do you want to know?"

"What does *kanga* mean?"

"It means hen. The first *kanga* to be made had white dots on a black background, which resembled the feathers of a hen."

"What about Swahili?" I asked, laughing.

"It means people of the coast."

"What about names?"

"Most of our names have meanings. My name, for example, means Luck."

"And what does Amani mean?"

He looked at me shyly, allowing a faint smile to touch his lips. "It means Peace," he said, glancing at Jungu as if for approval. "And what about your names," he asked. "Don't they have meanings? What does your name mean, for example?"

"Some of them have meanings, but most don't. Alinda means God is the protector."

We did not say anything for a long time until we heard voices carried towards us by the early morning breeze.

"I must go now," Bahati broke the silence.

"Thank you very much for the present," Jungu called after him as he disappeared behind the house, to the small path that would lead him to the shelters.

The voices belonged to Father and the old man. Father walked slightly ahead, often stopping for the old man to catch up with him. The old man walked with the aid of two crutches, the parts where his armpits rested were padded with pieces of the *kanga* that had previously bandaged his stump. Father asked Jungu to bring a chair for the old man. He sat down slowly, with obvious difficulty. The stump was uncovered, and the skin was beginning to grow back.

He looked thinner and older, since he had been bedridden for the past months. The flesh below his eyelids hung like an old piece of cloth. Jungu and I greeted him, asking after his health.

"I hear you've also been sick. How are you feeling now?" he asked me.

"She wasn't well yesterday," Father answered for me. "Nyin-abarongo told me you were vomiting again. And this morning you woke up late."

"Yes." I answered curtly, not wanting to remember the smell of blood lest I started vomiting again. "But I am fine now. Where are the others?" I asked Father.

"They passed through the fields to bring food for lunch—that is, if they can find any. These soldiers are eating everything that grows! Do you have anything left?" he turned to the old man.

"Very little, though they always ask for permission before they go into the fields. But what difference does it make? Very soon, we won't have anything to eat. The young one with a shy smile brings me two tins of beef every day, even though I told him I don't eat meat. You girls should come and collect them."

"I wish they would leave. Surely they've been here long enough!" Father said.

"It's been three months now," the old man said, looking down at his stump. "And it seems they'll be here for some more weeks—that's what I heard the young one say. Apparently, they are planning for a big battle up in the north where they suspect Amin is still hiding. It seems they are waiting for some more soldiers to join them."

Father sighed. Jungu looked at me sideways as if to ask: "Haven't you heard that?"

seventeen

"The Lendu woman is pregnant!" Nyinabarongo surprised us with the revelation one morning.

"But Kaaka used to say that she was barren!" Maya said, her voice laced with disbelief.

"Yes, I also believed so. I mean, they have lived here for almost ten years now, and she has never fallen pregnant before," Nyinabarongo said.

"And her husband is not here," Jungu added. "What will he say when he returns and finds her pregnant?"

"Who knows that he will come back?" Nyinabarongo sounded doubtful. "Most people who ran away have returned, since the war is almost over. Maybe he drowned in that deep river in Zaire while fishing. Who knows? Or perhaps he has decided to go back and live in that country for good."

"But what about his wife? He can't just abandon her?" Jungu sounded concerned.

"He has another wife in Zaire; that's what the Lendu woman told me. When they first met, he was much older than she. He was married and working in the laboratory at the hospital where the Lendu woman worked as a nurse-aid. He abandoned his first wife because she had failed to become pregnant, and he married the Lendu woman. But whenever he used to go back to Zaire to fish, he would stay with his first wife. Perhaps now he has decided to return to her for good."

"Did she tell you she was pregnant?" I asked Nyinabarongo.

"Yes, she did. She has also moved all her belongings to Uncle Kembo's house. That's where she lives now."

"And what about Uncle Kembo's wife? I mean, won't she come back when the war is over?" I asked.

"Maybe. She always talked of leaving him after he had abandoned her to live in town with those other wives. She never really accepted him back, but since it was his house . . ."

Tendo walked up silently to where we were sitting in the yard. He looked agitated and greeted us hurriedly. Maya tried to crack a joke, teasing him that he was now behaving like a soldier, even walking like one. He ignored her and beckoned me to follow him, saying that he had something important to tell me. He was holding a small plastic bag, which he kept shifting from one hand to another, as if its weight were a big burden to him.

"I didn't expect to see you here at this time of the day," I said, my tone accusing. "You've completely forgotten about us! You don't help us with the housework! You spend all your time with the Liberators. You know you are supposed to fetch milk for the baby. The man who used to supply us has no cows anymore. They've all been eaten by your friends, and now we have to fetch the milk from town, with the bicycle. It's a long distance. Maya has had to learn how to ride the bicycle, but it's dangerous to send her there alone, especially with all these soldiers roaming about. You have to come back and help us! And what will you do when they leave?"

"What are you two quarrelling about?" We had not heard Father walking towards us, and we knew he was there only when he spoke.

"Nothing," Tendo answered quickly. "I have to go now." He was getting agitated again.

"Tendo!" Father said sharply. "What's the matter with you? You have completely abandoned this home, you don't help out with anything at all! I'm warning you," Father pointed at him with his finger, like a gun, "if you continue with this kind of behavior, I will ask you to find another home."

Tendo turned and looked at Father briefly before walking off, a spring in his step, towards the path behind the kitchen.

"I've been to see their commander," Father said after a long silence, his lower lip quivering.

"About what?" it was Nyinabarongo who asked. She had walked to where I stood with Father.

"About Tendo," Father sighed. He looked tired.

"You should eat," Nyinabarongo suggested. "You left very early this morning without eating anything. Can I bring your breakfast?"

Father agreed, and Nyinabrongo called Maya, asking her to lay a place for Father in the kitchen. She asked me to warm his tea and food. When I had finished, I came outside and called Father to come and eat. He sat down heavily on the low stool, uncovered the food, and started eating quickly.

"I went to talk to their commander about Tendo," he said again, his mouth full. "I'm worried about him. He's so much taken up with them. That friend of his is even teaching him how to shoot a gun."

"Did you also talk to him about the issue of food?" Nyinabarongo asked. "Very soon we won't be able to afford two meals a day. Their commander should restrain them from eating our food! After all, they are supplied with their own—but they claim that our food here tastes better.

"Yesterday, when they came to ask me for food, I refused, and they offered to buy it from me. But what will I do with money? We can't eat the paper. There's nowhere to buy food!"

"That's another issue I talked to their commander about," Father said. "There are rumors that the soldiers have started taking people's money, not by force, but through persuasive begging. The villagers feel grateful that they liberated us from Amin and give them the money. Their commander has assured me that he will be checking each of them every night before they go to sleep, and anyone found with money on him will be asked to surrender it so that the commander can return it to the villagers."

"Let's hope they leave soon," Nyinabarongo sighed.

During the night, I was surprised to hear voices coming from the sitting room. I listened carefully and realized that they were those of the Lendu woman and Uncle Kembo.

I felt for Jungu's wristwatch, which she kept on the round table between our beds. I found it and moved closer to the window, where the moon lit up the room. It was five-thirty in the morning. How had the whole night slipped by!

"I heard some commotion and the sound of many people speaking in low voices," the Lendu woman was saying, "but when I listened again, I heard nothing, and I went back to sleep."

"Then I heard vehicles starting up and opened the door to see what was happening," Uncle Kembo added. "It is astonishing! They must have started packing soon after we went to bed. The whole place is cleared out. Nothing remains, only the empty cans of meat."

"I still can't believe they could leave just like that," Father said slowly.

"Well, apparently, they did. At least they should have informed me, the person who gave them space to build their shelters," Uncle Kembo said in a hurt tone.

Jungu turned in her bed. "Who are they talking about?" she whispered to me in the dark.

"The Liberators. They've left!"

"But Bahati didn't tell me! I was with him yesterday." She jumped out of bed and opened the door, heading for the sitting room. I also got out of bed, found a *kanga*, wrapped it around my nightdress, and followed her.

"Did Bahati also leave?" she asked no one in particular.

"They've all gone," Uncle Kembo replied.

"Tendo, too. He's nowhere to be seen. All his belongings are gone!" Father seemed to be in shock. He was holding his head in his hands.

Jungu looked stunned. The birds had begun to sing outside, and I heard the baby crying. Nyinabarongo joined us, holding him. No one said anything, and the minutes ticked by.

"Let's go back home," the Lendu woman said to Uncle Kembo. "I didn't lock the house, and with these . . . these people gone, who knows how secure we'll be."

Jungu walked back to the bedroom, and I followed her. She sat on the bed heavily. I opened one of the windows and peeped outside. A chill air touched my face, and I closed the window again.

"I'm sure Bahati left a message for me. I'm going to check in his shelter."

"It's still very cold outside. Why don't you wait for the sun to come up?"

"No!" Jungu shouted, her voice fierce. She turned and looked at me sullenly. "I want to know if he left any message. He can't just leave me behind like that! If there's no message, I'll still follow them. At least I know where they're heading to from here."

There was a knock at our window. I looked up suspiciously, wondering who it might be at this time of the morning. Jungu stared at me impatiently, but still I did not move. A second knock followed, this time a little louder than the first, and a faint whisper calling my name, then Jungu's. Jungu stood up and threw the window open. The birds that had been perching on the tree nearby fluttered away.

We heard the Lendu woman's voice. "Lock the door, girls. We don't know what's going to happen with our protectors gone."

"I'm sure Bahati left a message for me," Jungu said, as if trying to convince herself. "I'll even check in our special place where he used to take me whenever he wanted me to hold him."

As she spoke, she pulled on a dress on top of her nightdress. She retrieved a pair of shoes from under her bed, and, very swiftly, left the room.

At breakfast, Father did not say anything, nor did he eat. His face wore an expression of disbelief, and he was acting as though someone had died, as he had when Mother and Kaaka had died. Jungu had not returned, and Maya had gone wandering through the demolished shelters, to see if she could find anything of value. It was raining steadily, and after we had finished eating, I put the two big earthen pots outside to catch the rainwater. Some time later, Maya came back, holding a round metal object, gray in color.

"What have you got?" I asked her.

"Some money!" The awe in her voice was unmistakable. "It was hidden in a helmet. I took this helmet so I could use it when riding the bicycle, but as I was putting it on my head, the money fell out."

"Give it to Father. He will return it to the villagers."

"Can't we use it to buy some clothes for ourselves when the war is over? We don't have anything to wear."

"Father will buy what we need."

"But he's not working anymore. Do you think he'll go back to the city to work?"

"I don't know. I'm so tired, Maya. We woke up very early this morning. I am going back to sleep now."

When I entered the bedroom I shared with Jungu, I realized immediately that all her clothes were missing.

"Jungu is gone," I rushed to tell Father, who I found sitting alone in the sitting room.

"Gone where?" he asked, absentmindedly.

"I think she has followed them," I said, hesitant to tell him I knew for sure.

Father kept quiet. My mind was racing. I remembered what Mother had told me about people with mixed blood being suicidal. I started crying. Father moved over to where I stood and put his arms around me. I held on to him tightly.

"I will go and look for Jungu," he said. "Go to sleep, Alinda. You look tired."

I could not stop thinking about Jungu. She was my best friend, and of late, had become like a sister to me. And Tendo. Why didn't he tell me that he was planning to run away with the Liberators? Maybe that's what he had wanted to tell me yesterday when Father interrupted us. Suppose he was killed in the fighting? I stayed awake for a long time, waiting for Father to come and tell me that he had found Jungu. Nyinabarongo came to tell me that supper was ready, but I told her I did not feel like eating.

eighteen

A slight scratch on my window woke me. I opened my eyes, slowly raising my head from the pillow. The window was open. I must have forgotten to close it the previous evening. A heavy gray dawn met my eyes, its first faint light revealing the silhouette of a person.

"It's me," Bahati's voice came through the window.

"Bahati?" My voice must have portrayed the disbelief I felt at hearing his voice.

"Yes, I didn't leave with the rest of them. I hid in Kaaka's house. Where's Jungu?"

"She left! She said she was going to follow you."

"But I sent a message to her yesterday, through Tendo. Didn't he give it to her? It was written on a *kanga*, and I gave the *kanga* to Tendo to bring to her."

"I don't know, Tendo was in a hurry, and we did not talk much. He had a plastic bag but he must've forgotten to give it to Jungu."

"I told her I would never leave her. Didn't she believe me?"

"She was extremely hurt when she discovered you had left."

"I wouldn't leave her! I was going to ask your father to let us live in Kaaka's house—Jungu and me. It's empty. Do you think he will say yes?"

"I don't know."

"I want to live here with Jungu and have a family. Where do you think she headed?"

Suddenly, I felt very exhausted. Bahati's voice started fading away. I wanted him to go so I could sleep again. "You can talk to Father in the morning, Bahati," I said to him, but I don't think he heard me, for he had already started walking away.

nineteen

About a month after Jungu ran away to follow the Liberators, a powerful earthquake shook our house. I first felt the tremors when I got out of bed to urinate in the blue basin I kept under my bed. I thought the ground had opened up, and I quickly jumped back into bed without urinating.

The bed started moving, and I thought someone was under it trying to lift it off the ground. I screamed for help and held tightly onto the bedpost for support. Maya let out a piercing yell, and Nyinabarongo's child cried loudly.

Tea cups rattled in the cupboard, and the saucepans fell off the rack. The small table in my room where Jungu used to keep her wristwatch started moving towards the door, and the lamp on it fell and shattered on the ground. I screamed more loudly. Father was shouting to us to get out of the house. Suddenly, there was calm.

I continued lying in bed, a cold shiver running through my body. I heard Father open the front door, and I heard the others follow him. Maya was shouting my name, urging me to join them.

It was almost morning, judging from the faint patch of light that streamed in from the open door. Nyinabarongo appeared in the doorway and said, "Come outside, Alinda. It's over now. It won't come back. Don't be afraid."

I climbed out of bed with difficulty, placing my feet on the floor tentatively. Small needles seemed to pierce them as I walked outside to join the others. We stood in the yard, quiet except for Nyinabarongo, who was murmuring soothing words to her child. A cold wind blew towards us, and I shivered all the more. Heavy dark clouds hung in the sky, looking as though they might fall down on us at any time.

Bahati stood next to me, looking shaken.

"The walls of my house have cracked," he said to me, meaning Kaaka's house. "I think the house might fall down." His lower lip quivered as he spoke.

"Don't go back there," I said to him. "Come and sleep in our house. You can use Tendo's bedroom."

"This is the strongest earthquake we've experienced in many, many years," Father said, looking at Bahati. "It's . . ." He did not finish the sentence.

It started raining, then, a sudden, violent downpour. A fierce wind swept through the trees, causing the branches to sway wildly. We rushed back into the house and crowded together in the small sitting room. Father sat in his foldaway chair, his legs spread wide apart. The baby sat in his lap, kicking its feet vigorously.

"All this rain!" Maya broke the silence. "What does it want? It's been raining ever since the Liberators left," she continued, twisting her mouth in disapproval.

"And there's more to come," Nyinabarongo added.

"More rain?" Maya groaned.

"Well, all that shaking of Mother Earth's buttocks this morning is bound to earn her another beating from her husband, Heaven. He might think that she was trying to entice another lover with her big buttocks, and he's sure to send more of his messengers to beat her up," Nyinabarongo said seriously.

Maya and I laughed together. Bahati laughed very loudly, covering his face with his hands as if he were embarrassed. It was good to see him laugh. He seemed to have recovered from the experience of the morning's earthquake and of losing Jungu. Actually, this was the first time I had seen him laugh so loudly since his unsuccessful attempt to follow Jungu. Only Father did not laugh. I glanced at him briefly, noting the pain etched deeply in his eyes. He stood up and went to the cupboard at the end of the small corridor, where we sometimes kept leftover food. He came back with a piece of potato on a plate, broke off a tiny bit, mashed it, and put it into the baby's mouth. Nyinabarongo's child walked up to Father and stretched her hand to receive a piece too.

"You mean the earthquake has caused all this rain?" Maya asked Nyinabarongo. "But when it started raining, the earthquake hadn't passed by!" she reasoned.

"Maybe a lighter, female one came, but we didn't notice it," Nyinabarongo explained. "It might rain for the whole week," she went on, speaking slowly.

"A whole week! God. No!" Maya cried out.

"And very soon we won't have any firewood. We might have to think of cooking only one meal a day," Nyinabarongo went on in a worried tone.

It continued to rain without stop. Hailstones beat loudly on the roof, and we had stopped talking because we could not hear one another. There was a hole in the ridge where the thatch was joined, and rainwater seeped through easily. I placed a big saucepan directly below the hole. The water made a loud, rhythmic sound as it fell into the pan.

From the windows, we could see the destruction the storm was causing in the banana plantation. The stems were breaking in two, as if a madman had felled them. The leaves of the ones that remained standing had been shredded into small strips. Pools of water filled the ditches where the reed enclosure used to stand, before Amin's soldiers kicked it down.

It was late afternoon before the storm finally subsided, and outside it was already growing dark. Father talked of going to check on Uncle Kembo to see how he and the Lendu woman had survived the storm, but Nyinabarongo managed to persuade him to put off the visit until the next day. "Who knows what sorts of creatures the storm has unearthed? Do you want to step on poisonous earthworms?"

"Earthworms and millipedes have never bitten anyone," Father argued.

"There might be other creatures," Nyinabarongo warned. "Snakes, maybe. Who knows? Anyway, it's better you don't go out tonight."

It was a very cold night. At one point, I woke up and squeezed a piece of cloth between the spaces that separated the wooden shutters in my room, hoping to keep the cold air out. It took me a long time to fall asleep again, and I dreamed that the roof of our house had flown off, and that water was soaking my bed. I was swimming in a puddle of water, and I was going to drown and die! I woke up in a cold sweat and did not fall asleep again until daybreak.

Nyinabarongo came to call us very early. She said we had to fetch firewood and store it on the rack in the kitchen. My head felt heavy from lack of sleep, and my eyes felt as though salt had been rubbed into them.

Bahati was already standing in the yard, dressed in some of Tendo's clothes: a light blue pair of shorts and a pale yellow jersey with the words "Chicago Bulls" on the back. I started to say something to him but was interrupted by the arrival of Uncle Kembo. His face wore a dark expression, and he sounded agitated as he greeted us.

"Where's your father?" he asked us.

"What's the problem?" Father answered as he came to the front door. "I was about to come to your house to check how you survived the storm. Actually, I wanted to come last night but . . ."

"The Lendu woman's house is gone!" Uncle Kembo interrupted Father. "The walls just caved in and the . . ."

"Has it fallen down completely?"

"Yes. The iron sheets flew off and the walls collapsed."

"How terrible!" Nyinabarongo exclaimed, coming to stand near Father. "But at least she had removed all her valuables."

"What about the old man's?" Father asked worriedly. "We have to go and check on him."

"It survived," Uncle Kembo replied. "There isn't even a crack in the walls."

"How come?" Nyinabarongo sounded doubtful. "If I remember correctly, his was much weaker than the Lendu woman's because his bricks were made out of mere soil."

"That's right," Uncle Kembo agreed. "By the way, where did you put your iron sheets when you demolished your house? Are they still in good condition? We could use them to rebuild the Lendu woman's house."

"I don't think you should rebuild her house. She now has a new home–and a new life–with you. Let the old house go together with her old life."

Uncle Kembo looked thoughtful as he digested what Nyinabarongo had said. There was a long silence.

"We'll have to demolish Kaaka's house too," Father said at last. "The walls also gave in after that heavy rain yesterday."

"No. It's the earthquake," Nyinabarongo disagreed. "It caused all this rain!"

"We shouldn't complain about the rain, though," Father said. "At least we can now grow enough food to refill the granaries emptied by all we fed to the Liberators."

"Talking of the Liberators, all their shelters were washed away by the rain," Uncle Kembo informed us.

"Well, now we have nothing left to remind us of that painful era," Nyinabarongo said, sounding relieved.

"Except Bahati," Father corrected, glancing at him and dropping his voice to a whisper. "He's one of us now. I don't think he will try to follow the Liberators again after that terrible experience!"

"By the way, what exactly happened? I never got to know the whole story," Uncle Kembo asked.

"I warned Bahati that he would not be able to travel all the way to Arua alone. I mean, it is well over six hundred kilometers from here! Besides, the buses were not yet working. But he insisted. He boarded an old lorry that was carrying fishermen to Lake Albert, hoping to use that route. Just a little while later, the driver thought he saw soldiers who looked like Amin's. He panicked and jumped out of the running lorry. Bahati managed to escape with minor injuries, but two people died in that accident.

"Yesterday I went to the Liberators' offices again to check if they had any information on Jungu and Tendo," Father continued, after a prolonged silence.

"What did they say?" Uncle Kembo asked, a trace of hope detectable in his voice.

"No news. No news at all," Father shook his head. "I don't know how to explain this to Jungu's mother. That child was under my care when she disappeared."

"I am sure she will understand," Nyinabarongo said. "After all, your own son, too, disappeared. Perhaps they will both return after the war is over."

twenty

Father left for the city soon after the rains stopped. This was the longest period he had stayed with us as far back as I could remember. When he first arrived, the baby was not yet born, and now he was almost five months old. We walked with Father up to the Center, which was about three kilometers from our home. There he would catch the bus to the city. Maya carried a chicken, wrapped in banana leaves, Bahati carried a small sisal bag, which contained fresh food, I carried the baby, and Nyinabarongo carried her child on her back. Uncle Kembo walked a little ahead of us, not talking, and the Lendu woman carried a plastic bag on her head containing millet flour.

People and calm seemed to have returned to the Center, which had been deserted because of the presence of Amin's soldiers. The small kiosks that sold fruit and other kinds of food were open, and so was the big shop, which usually sold pieces of cloth brought from Zaire. The market, where the Lendu woman's husband used to sell fish was also open, and it was busy with many buyers and sellers moving about.

People who recognized Father came to where we were standing to greet him, some offering their sympathies about the deaths in our family. A young man who was selling tape cassettes tried to persuade Father to buy a cassette of Congolese music.

He inserted it into the big radio he carried and pressed "play." Loud, squeaky music filled the air. Father waved him away, saying he was not interested in the cassette.

There was no place to sit, since the wooden benches and the tree stumps were wet from the heavy rains. Maya wanted us to sit on a long bench on the big shop's verandah, but Father said the bus driver would not see him there when he waved.

We had to remain standing near the junction of the three roads. One led to Zaire, via Lake Albert, the same road Amin's soldiers had used as their exit route. The second led to the city, while the third led to the big tea plantation, which used to be owned by the Indians.

The warm morning sun caressed our faces and bare arms. Blossoming trees lined the roadside, and the scents of yellow hibiscus and white violets filled the air. Crickets made loud, high-pitched chirps. One or two cars passed by, heading to the tea plantation.

Father said jokingly to us, "Now, I'm confident that you won't be washed away by the rains. You have a man who can take care of you," he said, patting Bahati's shoulder.

"I will take care of them," Bahati said with assurance, flexing his shoulders.

"Maya, be a good girl," Father continued, fondly stroking Maya's ears.

His mood had lightened, and there was noticeable laughter in his voice. It was Maya who seemed to have assumed Father's gloomy mood. She hadn't said anything as we had walked to the Center.

"When will we go back to school?" she asked Father.

"Soon," Father replied, "as soon as the new term begins. I'll be back then and will see to your school requirements."

"Really!" Maya said excitedly. "Alinda, aren't you happy to be going back to school? You act as though you don't care at all!" Her tone was reproachful.

"But what about the baby?" I said the first thing that came to my mind.

"Oh, don't worry about that," Father said with a little laugh. "He has a new mother now," he added, pointing to Nyinabarongo.

Nyinabarongo smiled reassuringly and nodded her head.

"I will assist too," the Lendu woman added. Her pregnancy was visible through the *kanga* she had wound round her waist. She gave the plastic bag to Father, and he thanked her.

We heard the bus approaching. Father turned to Bahati, "And you too will be starting school with the others."

A wide grin spread across Bahati's whole face, lingering there for a while, before he broke into a contented chuckle.

Uncle Kembo drew nearer to where Father was standing and clasped both his hands in a firm grip. "Travel safely, and don't forget to write to us."

Father nodded. "I will. And keep well too."

afterword

Goretti Kyomuhendo was born in 1965 in the district where *Waiting* is set, in the town of Hoima in western Uganda. She went to school there, and then, after passing exams at the highest school-leaving level, she studied Marketing at the National College of Business Studies, Nakawa (now part of Makerere University). She has always been interested in writing, and after publishing her first novel, she became the first woman writer from Uganda to attend the International Writing Program at the University of Iowa, in 1997. In 2004–2005, Kyomuhendo studied for a Master's degree in Creative Writing at the University of KwaZulu-Natal in South Africa; the first draft of *Waiting* was successfully submitted for the degree in 2005.

Waiting is Kyomuhendo's fourth novel for adult readers (she has also written two novels for children: *Different Worlds* [1998] and *Hare and the King's Cow* [2006]). Her previous books were all published in Uganda, and unfortunately, because of the difficulties of book distribution in Africa, they are not readily available outside her country. They show that even before Kyomuhendo wrote *Waiting*, she had achieved considerable stylistic range in representing the troubled, and often turbulent, lives of her women protagonists.

Kyomuhendo's first novel, *The First Daughter* (1996), examines patriarchal attitudes to women and how these govern their options in contemporary Uganda. It is an account of a young girl whose father's pride in her leads to his unusual decision to send her to school. (A daughter, unlike a son, was not usually considered worth the cost of formal schooling because, once she had married, she would leave the parental home, and her education would serve her new, marital family.) When, in her senior year, she becomes pregnant, she finds herself rejected by her father, and apparently abandoned by her lover. Eventually, she is reunited with the man she loves, and with a degree in law as her safeguard, she marries him, confident that she and her child will find happiness.

Secrets No More (1999) follows this novel. After opening with the massacres in Rwanda, which are presented as a consequence of male aggression and rivalry fueled by ethnic conflict, this story follows the main character, Marina, to Uganda. Although there is peace in this country there, the focus is again on a young woman's suffering at the hands of domineering and often brutal men. Like *The First Daughter*, this novel also maintains a belief in good men, and it presents Marina's happiness as secured when she finds a suitable man to care for her. Both novels work in the romantic mode in order to present issues that are of perennial concern to African women: marriage, children, and trustworthy men.

The third novel for adults that Kyomuhendo published is *Whispers from Vera* (2002). This book began as a column in *The Crusader*, one of two Kampala-based newspapers for which she wrote regular columns at the time (the other was *The Monitor*).[1] Its narration departs from the third-person mode of the other two books and tells its story through the chatty letters that Vera writes as she confides in an unnamed friend. *Whispers* also marks a dramatic change in the possibilities envisaged for women; its characters are sophisticated, urban women, who enjoy their sexuality and no longer feel alone and helpless when they meet male aggression, or patriarchal power, or both. However hurt they may be, they are prepared to look after themselves by becoming materially and emotionally independent.

In *Waiting*, Kyomuhendo's art takes on yet another dimension as she develops her lyrical powers to write a narrative in which no word is superfluous, in which one character's point of view dominates, and in which much of the story unfolds through dialogue. In Ugandan fiction, this short novel is unique in its delicate and generally low-keyed representation of the horrifying experiences of ordinary villagers caught in a war. Kyomuhendo's small but heterogeneous cast finds itself in the path of Idi Amin's fleeing soldiers as his regime in Uganda collapses in 1979. Amin's soldiers were mostly northerners, and they were fleeing in order either to melt into the population of their home areas or to cross Lake Albert into the Democratic Republic of Congo (DRC). The village in *Waiting* is located in Hoima district, near Lake Albert in the western Rift Valley that forms one of Uganda's borders, and it lies directly in the path of the soldiers' disorderly flight northwards.

Waiting joins a growing number of novels from East Africa that depict post-independence, internal, and cross-border wars. After independence in 1962, Ugandans were subjected to constant power struggles as the newly created nation-state began to fracture along ethnic lines. The then Prime Minister, Milton Obote, first assumed sole power and suspended the constitution in 1966; he was ousted in a military coup headed by Idi Amin in 1971, who was in turn ousted by combined Ugandan and Tanzanian forces in 1979, which enabled Obote to return in 1980. He ruled until 1985 (a period now known as "Obote 2"). In 1986, Museveni entered Kampala at the head of a liberation army; he had led a five-year guerilla war against Obote during which fighting was concentrated in the region known as the Luweero Triangle, north of Kampala. After difficult negotioations, which included the passing of a new constitution, the current President, Yoweri Museveni, assumed power. The first presidential elections were held in 1996. *Waiting* depicts a small part of this troubled history; a fuller representation of it is given in Moses Isegawa's celebrated novel, *Abyssinian Chronicles* (2000). But what distinguishes Kyomuhendo's novel is her decision to focus on humble village lives that are far removed from the centers of power, and to use the observations of a young girl who is just reaching adolescence to depict the suffering of a group of people. No other Ugandan writer has used the perceptions of a young girl who, at a time in her life when she would normally be beginning to comprehend how her family's practices sustain the proper functioning of her world, is compelled to try to make sense of unpredictable violence against which, as she witnesses it, none of the villagers can protect themselves.

Waiting is not the first novel in which Kyomuhendo has written about power struggles that erupt into war. As indicated above, *Secrets No More* opens during the genocide in Rwanda in the early 1950s: the protagonist sees her Tutsi mother raped and killed by an army officer she had thought was a friend, and then the young girl has to watch from her hiding place as her younger sisters and brother are summarily killed by the group of Hutu soldiers he is commanding. Other women writers too are beginning to depict the brutalities of conflict in the region from the point of view of women characters. For example, Monica Arac de Nyeko sets her short story, "Strange Fruit" (2005), in the Kitgum region of northern Uganda where a group that calls itself the Lord's Resistance Army has been engaged in an armed rebellion against the government,[2] and she uses the point of view of a young wife to recount the horrific killing of her husband who had been forcibly marched away by the rebels to fight, and had then fled back home, only to be tortured and killed by state soldiers looking for the rebels.

Since its inception ten years ago, Kyomuhendo has been the convenor of FEMRITE (Uganda Women Writers' Association). This group began meeting in 1995 when a few women who wanted to "make the voice of the female writer . . . more present in the Ugandan literary scene"[3] met in the office of Mary Karooro Okurut in the literature department of Makerere University. In a brief reference to her reasons for starting this group, Okurut explains that from the Amin years until about 1986, very little literature was produced in Uganda. Then, although things began to change (she says that in the 1990s, Fountain Publishers in Kampala published two of her plays, as well as a novel by Lillian Tindyebwa), "I realized that there were many women with manuscripts which were stashed away. Several of these had been with publishers for more than ten years and had no chance of being published. There were also very many potential women writers who needed encouragement, thus the birth of FEMRITE" (Okurut 2000: 76–77). The other women at that first meeting were not necessarily aspiring novelists; they included Monica Barya Chibita (a journalist, who suggested the name "'FEMRITE'"), Shirley Byakutaga (a linguist), Rosemary Kyarimpa (a novelist), Susan Kiguli (a poet), and Goretti Kyomuhendo. When the association was formally launched in May 1996 as a voluntary grouping that would encourage and train aspirant writers, Kyomuhendo was elected as an executive member.

There are currently about 28 members who constitute the general assembly of FEMRITE and who meet monthly at the FEMRITE offices, which are housed on Kiira Road in Kamwokya, a suburb of Kampala. The organization is a vigorous, ambitious, and successful one: it meets weekly in the Association's offices, and at these workshops, members discuss each other's work in progress. These meetings are open to non-members and attract male as well as female writers.

In its efforts to create a readership in Uganda, the Association also hosts a radio talk-show on *Monitor FM* every Saturday evening, during which listeners are encouraged to air their views about books that they have read and about literature in general. It likewise helped to launch a program on Uganda Television called "The Writers' Dawn." This program features published writers who read from and discuss their recent work. A book page in the government newspaper, *The New Vision*, was started partly through FEMRITE's efforts. In 1997, FEMRITE began a quarterly magazine called *New Era*, which featured discussions of women's position in society; this has since been replaced by a more literary journal, *Word Write*, which includes essays and creative work by Ugandan writers—men as well as women. The organization's most ambitious project each year is a week-long celebration of women's writing at which the main focus is the "importance of books to a developing country like Uganda." The Ghanaian writer Ama Ata Aidoo was the first celebrity speaker in 2000, and in 2006 (FEMRITE's tenth anniversary, which was celebrated from July 17–21, 2006) the guests were Dr. Jane Plastow from Leeds University, England, and the novelist Akachi Adimora Ezeigbo from Nigeria. The donors, HIVOS in the Netherlands, were also represented. Each year, during this week, the guest writers run workshops for local writers and give public interviews and readings from their work. Moreover, and perhaps more important than all of these other activities, FEMRITE started a small publishing venture that, by 2006, had issued 14 titles, including novels, short stories, and poetry.[4]

As FEMRITE's chief administrative officer, Kyomuhendo has been responsible for fundraising and reporting to the funders, for promoting FEMRITE's image, for preparing work plans and budgets, and for marketing and publicizing the books that the Association publishes. Besides encouraging women to write by running workshops and by maintaining a small resource center with the help of the British Council and the American Center in Kampala, FEMRITE provides something of a home away from home for women who are experiencing trouble in their personal lives, and many of these women work in a voluntary capacity for the organization. In his brief survey of Ugandan literature, Austin Bukenya concludes with a discussion of the heartening revival of writing since 1986, and he says: "The advent of the Uganda Women Writers' Association [FEMRITE] and its associated publishing wing has led to a productivity in Ugandan writing which is likely to affect the whole writing and reading culture of the country" (2000: xix).

In its efforts to create a public space, a site of utterance from which the various experiences and views of women can be presented and received with respect, FEMRITE has chosen a political task demanding courage and resilience. By insisting that women can speak with authority and should be listened to, its members are calling into question the patriarchal assumption that power in society should be held only by men. This is a profound challenge to practices that have held sway for so long that to many people they seem not only right but natural. Almost 25 years ago, Simon Gikandi said that "all East African novels have politics as their motive force. The way of feeling and seeing politics . . . may vary . . . but always, it is how politics affect the physical and psychological experience that matters most to these novelists" (1984: 232). Gikandi was commenting on politics in the sense of a resistance to the "colonial experience" (1984: 233) that was fueling nationalism in East African countries. Two generations later his observation may still be felt to be true of Ugandan writing, but this time with reference to two senses of "politics." First, there is a continuing resistance to colonialism in that the abuses of power by three successive presidencies (Obote, Amin, and Obote again) were all in part shaped by its legacy. Secondly, there is the new, and perhaps even more fundamental, meaning of "politics" that is evident in Ugandan writing, particularly in novels by Ugandan women, and that is the questioning of a gendered allocation and exercise of power.[5]

Susan Kiguli instances a recently published anthology, *Tears of Hope: A Collection of Short Stories by Ugandan Rural Women* (Wangusa and Barungi 2003) as an example of FEMRITE's pioneering work in giving voice to ordinary women and, in this case, to rural women. These stories are not fictional, but are accounts of actual experiences of and struggles against abuse told by women in interviews; each of their stories was then shaped and translated into English by a woman writer. The stories expose the "injustices imposed on . . . women by the strong patriarchal system in Uganda," and their recurring themes are, Kiguli says, "belonging, rejection . . . by the clans, domestic violence, desolation caused by the AIDS scourge, unfair divorce laws, women on women violence, and the oppressive attitudes on bride-price and land inheritance." The focus in this and other FEMRITE publications is not, however, simply on women as suffering victims, for, as Kiguli notes, the "theme of women's ability to survive and fight to make their own decisions" is what dominates. Novels published under the FEMRITE imprint are changing the image of women in Ugandan fiction and society as they explore issues from the point of view of women characters and establish the agency of women. This is a process that has been felt to be both "radical and subversive."

Kyomuhendo's second novel, *Secrets No More*, ran into the kind of controversy that can gather around women who presume to speak out in public; it was criticized as pornographic for its direct depictions of violence and sexual passion. In Uganda, as in many African societies, "discussion of sex in public was tabooed" and, as is the case elsewhere, these taboos often operate against women rather than men. As Kiguli points out, many novels by male writers in Africa depict sexual passion but have not been accused of being pornographic. This includes novels such as Mongo Beti's *The Poor Christ of Bomba* and Ferdinand Oyono's *Houseboy*, which are actually prescribed for schools in Uganda. Apparently, it is only when women write on such matters that people raise objections. It is not only the inconsistency of these accusations that is unjust; it is also that in the excited controversy that inevitably follows when sexual matters are in question, the other serious issues about which a writer such as Kyomuhendo invites her readers to think—issues such as ethnic conflict, violence, corruption, tyranny, exile, and betrayal—are overlooked. The controversy also hides the fact that writers are depicting the kind of events that have actually happened; it seems that, in the case of women writers, social taboos may silence the messenger without deterring offenders from the abhorrent act itself. Kiguli suggests that such misguided controversy, which disregards what is really serious in the work of women writers, is a symptom of "the largely repressive and violent politics, the male dominated cultural system and the constant changes resulting from colonial and post-colonial events" in Uganda.

In *Waiting*, Kyomuhendo turns once more to the impact of war and violence on ordinary people. How has she chosen to depict the violence of "a male dominated cultural system" and war's destruction of the fabric of life? How might her style reveal her response to public rejection of a woman writer's right to make issues such as violence, warfare, and oppression the subject of her fiction? Part of the answer lies in the way Kyomuhendo draws her reader into the atmosphere of half-submerged fear and uncertainty that opens and pervades her novel; another lies in the poignancy of her characters' turning to traditional wisdom amidst circumstances that are bringing about its destruction;[6] and a third lies in the gravitas that she gives to the routines of daily rural life. Above all, she portrays the quiet, unsentimental pathos of a small group of people who try to continue to care for one another amidst the devastations of war.

Rather than introducing her readers to the action through an explanatory account of the fighting, Kyomuhendo steps directly but delicately into the daily lives of her fictional family, thereby drawing her readers unarmed, as it were, into the line of fire. Her narrative method is more unobtrusive and probably more affecting than sustained exposition or dramatic confrontation would be. The opening scene, in which the young central figure, Alinda, and her family eat their evening meal, is both charming and filled with unstated tensions and fears. It is what remains unsaid that draws us in and holds us in suspense as the scene-painting is restricted to the immediate, and as the characters' remarks contain only the slightest of hints by which we might orient ourselves and assess what is happening. When Kaaka (the grandmother)[7] reminds Alinda's pregnant mother that she might have to "run" that night (4), lurking danger is evident, but who or what it is, and why it is, remains unstated. The characters know a little about these matters, but the reader knows nothing, yet. And as the scene unfolds, it is clear that the silences also reflect the family's own ignorance of the larger causes of the horror that is being visited upon them. The uncertainty that we feel mirrors the fears of the characters themselves, making Kyomuhendo's chosen mode one of subtle seduction that renders overt resistance or repudiation difficult. If "to read is to struggle to name" (Barthes 1974: 92), then a reader who cannot immediately name what is being presented will also find it difficult to bring preconceptions and stereotypes to bear, and will "struggle" to be judgmental and to repudiate. It is not until Chapter 2, when Alinda's father rides his bicycle to the nearby "trading Center,"[8] that we learn something of the larger context, but our knowledge is still limited to what the village characters themselves can find out. In this way, we discover that the pillaging men with guns who raid the villages at night are the remnants of Idi Amin's army: aggressively fearful soldiers who have been left to find their own way to places in the north where they will feel safe, and who plunder and murder as they move under cover of darkness.

As the family waits for the last of the soldiers to pass through their district, and then for the liberation forces to reach them, ordinary life is more or less held in abeyance. And yet the daily routines have to continue somehow, and on this "somehow,"the narrative focus rests. The practical tasks and obligations of each day, its small jokes and its familiar irritations, are what is recorded. In addition, precious belongings must be buried to hide them from the marauding soldiers, and the family must retreat to the bushes at the edge of the nearby plantation to sleep. At the same time, there are household chores to be undertaken: food, for example, must be prepared, and as Alinda carries out these tasks, she feels the obligation to instruct her younger sister, Maya, in the family's tried and trusted methods. Alinda herself is guided by the older women, who have a ready story or proverb that will explain or sanction each small event. Thus, Kaaka remarks that a falling leaf heralds a visitor from afar and that an unborn baby with too much hair will cause heartburn (4). Nyinabarongo confirms the legend that the moon bears the sun's children and explains that there are actually two such children in the sky (7). Even Alinda rebukes her impatient, interfering brother with a proverb: "those who ask what they know are looking for laughter" (31). And overarching the significance of the daily tasks and proverbial wisdom in time of war is the fact of the mother's pregnancy: a new life has been created, and must be defended with even more fervor amidst an orgy of killing. Their recognition of the demands of a new life, as well as their witnessing of the frailty of all life, causes the adults to feel the gravity of their situation keenly, but the children can still find it possible to be playful amidst the messy ending of a war, as when Tendo amuses himself by giving a false alarm from his perch in a tree. Alinda herself only half understands her parents' fears and gradually comes to realize that she might lose everything in a second; but then, everyone can relax enough to laugh a little when Mother confesses that the beans they are eating for supper give her wind.

One of the consequences of having marauding groups of soldiers pass through their area is that the people who gather each night to sleep in the bushes on the edge of the banana plantation where Alinda and her family live are not all blood relations; rather they are villagers drawn together in search of mutual protection. This enables Kyomuhendo to touch lightly on issues of ethnicity and cultural diversity—Uganda is a country of some 40 languages (the number depends on one's definition of a language) that fall into four or five main language groups (Knappert 1987: 205)[9]—and on some of the history that has shaped the small community she creates. We see how they draw on their customs and attitudes as they make the often difficult choices that are needed to hold their lives together.

For example, the woman who is known only by her ethnic identity, the Lendu woman, is from Zaire (now the DRC), and her husband has gone back there to obtain fish that he sells in the area from the Congo River system. Because she is a stranger, from a people said to eat monkeys, suspicion falls readily on her when Alinda's newborn brother is found to have *ebino*.[10] What saves her from the father's growing hostility and accusations of witchcraft is her gift of sugar for the nursing child; in return, she takes the opportunity to tell her story. She explains that she knows about the medicinal properties of herbs through having worked in wartime in a hospital in Zaire (53–54) that had no Western medicines.

Nyinabarongo, whose name has been given to her by the villagers in some derision, and means "mother of twins" although she has not actually borne twins, is also an outcast. Her husband's family has chased her away, and at first, she is tolerated by this group only because she might be useful to Alinda's pregnant mother. After the mother's death, however, and as the puny, newborn child hovers between life and death, she becomes useful in new ways, and ultimately she finds her place in Alinda's father's bed.

This union, like that between Uncle Kembo and the Lendu woman, does not represent the desperate grasping of pleasure by people about to die; it can be seen as life-sustaining, one of the realistic and practical compromises that members of a group must make in order to protect their number against external predators. When her friend Jungu tells Alinda about her father's new union, Alinda makes no comment, not even one of surprise or grief that her mother seems to have been so quickly forgotten. This is partly because the respect due to adults would not permit any overt comment and partly because even the children understand that life must go on and new choices must be made. In a social system where the family group is defined by both kinship and pragmatic considerations, an overt grief would be considered a self-indulgent luxury. Again, deeply as Alinda's father suffers when his son, Tendo, runs off to join the liberating forces, he remains stoical; and then, when the newcomer, Bahati, indicates by his behavior that he wants to become part of this re-grouping family, Alinda's father accepts the young foreigner into his son's role. As Bahati's reliable presence enables the father to return to his job in the distant city, he, in return, is given the promise of formal schooling. In a part of the continent where displaced people are counted in millions, this is (however ironic) an important indication from Kyomuhendo that war's destruction of settled communities can also make it possible for strangers, including foreign refugees, to find a place in the newly forming communities.

If the family's restructuring is one of the novel's most touching ways of recognizing how ordinary people cope with the disasters of war, then the young peoples' brief discussions of language in Chapters 15 and 16 offer a similarly delicate but penetrating glimpse of the reshaping of identities and the re-drawing of personal maps that can come about through the transnational aspect of war. When Alinda meets Bahati and hears Jungu's efforts to speak his language, Kiswahili, she seems to come to life, to wake up and begin to ask questions about the world beyond her own beleaguered village. Her exploration of linguistic differences stands in stark contrast to her first, brutal encounter with a foreign tongue, which occurred when she heard the fleeing soldiers demanding "women, food, and money" (37) and saw them kill her grandmother. In that encounter with Kiswahili, Uncle Kembo had to translate for those in hiding, and could do so because he was comparatively a man of the world, having converted to Islam during Amin's regime, owned a shop, married urban women, and spent time in Hoima town. Now Alinda asks questions about other languages and their relation to identity because she wants to know how people can make contact with each other across divisions that had, just a short time before, meant only death. These transnational linguistic exchanges are the novel's greatest sign of hope for the future, a hope that is relevant to present circumstances in Uganda as well as to the fiction's historical context.

While the novel presents language as the primary means of creating mutual understanding once fighting has ended, the wartime function of language is to mark the boundaries across which antagonists may combat one another. In the Great Lakes region of Africa, war is usually a transnational affair.[11] Although outsiders might see the ousting of Idi Amin as a purely Ugandan concern, the past five decades of constant fighting across the whole region indicate the wider, neo-colonial interests that are at stake. While Tanzania openly took part in the liberating of Uganda from Amin,[12] this process had repercussions in many of the other countries that border on Uganda. And these ripple effects had their origins at least a century earlier when many of the "countries" of the region were created and then formally colonized during and after the horse-trading by the European powers who carved up Africa at the notorious conference in Berlin in 1884. In the move towards Uganda's independence during and following World War II, "[m]ilitant nationalists had one fatal weakness. While they were able to rally workers and peasants to the political arena by putting forth popular demands, they could not give the resulting movement a clear direction" (Mamdani 1983: 17). The lack of cohesion enabled the departing colonial authority to push the "national question . . . of exploitation and oppression . . . into the background while bringing the nationality question [the divisive issues of nationality, race, and religion] into the foreground" (20). Phares Mutibwa, in his careful assessment of the problems faced by the first post-independence government in Uganda in 1962, points out that the constitution that had been negotiated in London entrenched divisions that were largely ethnic, and that it seemed to favor the Baganda over other peoples of the country (1992: 24).

As she begins to explore the meaning of language difference and its bearing on identity, Alinda works from her first language, which would be Runyoro, the main language of the Banyoro people of Hoima district. The song that she dreams her dead mother is singing, in Chapter 8, is in Runyoro;[13] as the text tells us, it was one of Kaaka's favorite songs, perhaps because it confirmed her own sense of the difficult cultural changes, in this case in the customs of dress, brought about by colonization. While Alinda knows that people in her country speak different languages, and while she has begun to learn English at school, there would have been little occasion for a child like her to encounter any of the other indigenous languages of Uganda. She might not even have heard Luganda, the language of the Baganda people whose ancient kingdom had its center at Kampala, which became the most important language alongside English during the colonial period. Thus, when her friend Jungu takes Alinda to meet some of the liberating army from Tanzania, Alinda knows little about them or their languages. She has yet to learn much of the geo-politics and history that a child her age—even a village child—would, in normal circumstances, already be taking for granted: that many people in Africa use an official national language, or communicate in a lingua franca, as well as speaking a first language from their region;[14] that in East Africa, a knowledge of English is not the only sign of formal education;

and that language may be ceasing to be the primary marker of a person's identity. These are lessons about language and identity, signaled in particular when the children explore the meanings of their names, that she learns rapidly and with pleasure when she meets Bahati and hears Kiswahili under utterly different circumstances from her first encounter with it. Now, thanks to the beautiful *kanga* that Bahati has brought with him from Tanzania and the politeness that the liberating forces are careful to extend to the villagers, Kiswahili can be recognized as one of the languages of friendship and love, instead of only death.

Although it is never sensational in its presentation of war, brutality, and death, *Waiting* is often shocking. The soldier's callous, unnecessary shooting of Kaaka brings to a head the dread that has pervaded the first section of the novel. The second section opens with Alinda's mother's death—a death undoubtedly brought about by the soldiers' presence, although the difficult childbirth might possibly have killed her in peacetime too. But a wholly unexpected shock erupts when the old man steps on a landmine left on a footpath by the fleeing soldiers. This accident not only brings home the horrors of war; it also allows us to register in passing the gendered differences in the villagers' responses to disaster. As might be expected, it is the Lendu woman who takes charge of the wounded man, but, and this is at first surprising, neither Father nor Uncle Kembo are capable of helping her when, for example, the old man has to be held down for rough-and-ready surgery. Although Father was ready to take up a panga against the soldiers in defense of his homestead and family, when it comes to caring for the wounded—or even for an ailing person, as is evident in his clumsiness when his sickly infant son has to be treated (50)—he, like the other men, cannot cope. This is not a rigidly gendered pattern, for Alinda too collapses when she has seen more blood than she can bear, but it indicates much about the behaviors and capacities inculcated in women and men.

The terrible accident that befalls the old man is also used to make us entertain the idea that even in a village in thrall to the arbitrary violence of a routed army, there is perhaps still some room for poetic justice. When the old man's story is eventually told to Alinda, it emerges that he has a terrible crime on his conscience, and, until the end, he is haunted by the memory of the wife he had killed. The fact that he has committed this crime may also be why, at the novel's conclusion, it feels appropriate that the earthquake and torrential rain that destroy so many of the village buildings associated with the past leave his home untouched, as though his life cannot be washed clean again.

The story that is told to Alinda about the old man, and that explains her mother's aversion to him, is only one of many such personal histories that are recounted to her. Together they form a reminder that this is a novel about a largely oral community in which stories are still the vital repository of history, and in which story-telling is the means of accounting for both the bonds and the ruptures that exist between individual people as well as whole societies. Kyomuhendo's narrative mode is mostly dialogue, and this underwrites the importance of story-telling, for it is usually Alinda's questioning that elicits one of these stories. Intertwined in these life-histories is material that readers might be inclined to categorize as myth or legend rather than history, but Kyomuhendo presents this as a material factor in her characters' lives, and thus something that cannot be placed simply in the symbolic realm. Kaaka's death is the occasion for a story that might pose particular challenges to a reader's interpretative experience. On her being wounded and killed, her family discovers that her distended stomach contains an unborn child. Later, when Nyinabarongo (who has largely taken over Kaaka's function as the authoritative source of folk wisdom)[15] assures Alinda that it was a "real baby" (58), she tells her the story of how Kaaka's mother had had the pregnancy made "invisible" so that Kaaka could safely be married without bringing shame to her family. But, socially desirable as marriage might have seemed, it also meant that Kaaka's community would be denied the healing powers that she had acquired by securing in her *kanga* the "fluids from [the] . . .

mating." of two snakes. Gain is set against loss, and the preserved but unborn child can perhaps be understood to symbolize this difficult equation. At this level, we can also recognize an indication that people's pasts may live on in them. Just as the old man can never eat meat and is still haunted by the wife he had killed, so Kaaka carries in her the child that she had longed to bear, but that was denied her when she and her mother were transgressors against two different and possibly conflicting sets of rules. But what Kaaka carried is a real child and not just the memory of a child. Nyinabarongo does not answer Alinda's question, "how could it have lived there for so long?"; nevertheless, this mysterious sign of Kaaka's desire and her punishment is one that we must respect as material reality in the world of *Waiting*, and as such, it is a sign to which not all cultures can give meaning (58).

As with Chenjerai Hove's novel *Bones* (1988), about the aftermath of war in Zimbabwe, one of the most striking features of *Waiting* is that it has no plot in the Aristotelian sense of there being a protagonist whose initial action gives rise to a chain of events in which the consequences and meaning of the initial act are worked out. The agent here is war, and what is required of Kyomuhendo's characters, men as well as women, is that they survive as best they can. What then of their agency, particularly women's agency that has been so important to the writers of FEMRITE? Here the novel's title and its narrative point of view come into play, for they serve to remind us that it is Alinda's emergence into the adult world that has been halted by the arrival of soldiers in her village. Kyomuhendo's lyrical art is such that we, rather than Alinda, feel this loss or denial at every turn. *Waiting* is thus a bildungsroman that has yet to happen. And this somewhat reactive condition seems right for Alinda in as much as questioning the material, psychological, and spiritual effects of war is not what young characters do in times of external crisis. Rather, these questions and reflections are what a reader must derive from thinking about Alinda's circumstances. At the same time, these matters are gathered under the thematic title of "waiting," and this word carries a connotation of expectations that have been suspended rather than terminated. Accordingly, the endurance of the victims is not all that readers are offered. For most of the five months in which we interact with Alinda and her family group, it is true that they can do little more than to endure, to survive. And so the narrating time of their "waiting" is filled by the daily routines and their interruption by the nightly visitations of the soldiers and then by the narration of the stories that Alinda is told of the past lives of some of the members of her enlarged family group. But, as I have suggested, with the eventual arrival of the liberating forces, glimpses of a possible change are given. Alinda's world begins to enlarge as she thinks about the implications of other languages and as her family group changes. When Tendo and Jungu run away with the departing Tanzanian soldiers, Alinda's life is depleted again, but it also gains Bahati for comparably pragmatic reasons to those which guided their earlier acceptance of Nyinabarongo.

Readers who know something of the history of Uganda after the fall of Idi Amin will be able to supply another dimension to the theme of "waiting" and to the delicate balancing of loss and gain to which the novel attends. Their text-external knowledge that Amin's regime was replaced by a weaker and more brutal government, with Milton Obote at its head, and that his fall was brought about by a further five years of civil war, will give a bitter-sweet edge to the subdued note of hope as the patterns of daily life seem to be restored at the end of *Waiting*. Kyomuhendo, of course, knows the history of her country from the inside; her not indicating what was to happen after the close of her story is not a sign of her neglect of history, but rather of her respect for historicity and for the point of view and knowledge of the young woman, Alinda, through whom she chose to relate one small but telling aspect of the wars that have troubled her country for almost four decades.

M.J. Daymond
University of KwaZulu-Natal, Durban
September 2006

NOTES

1. In *The Crusader*, the story ran between 1996–1998 under the title "From Vera to Assumpta," Assumpta being the sister who lives in the village and is renamed Jacinta in the novel. She becomes a character in the novel, and is not the narratee, who is simply addressed as "you."

2. The first leader of a rebellion in the north was a woman prophetess, Alice Lakwena. Her movement was strongest in the Acholi district, but after about a year, her followers were defeated, and she escaped to Kenya. A man claiming to be related to her, Joseph Kony, emerged as the next leader. In 1991, he named his group the Ugandan Peoples' Democratic Christian Army, and more recently, it became the Lord's Resistance Army. He seems to have few voluntary followers and to acquire most of his fighters by kidnapping children, who are made to carry out atrocities against the people in whose name the rebellion began. Kony's cause is now obscure, but it seems to have begun in a refusal to accept the result of the "rigged" election that brought Museveni to power in 1986 (Pirouet 1995; "Africa's Most Wanted" 2006: 42).

3. Most of the information about FEMRITE in this section has been taken from an article by Susan Kiguli. The quotations are from her typescript, which was then translated for publication in a book in Germany. The English translation of the book is forthcoming from Africa World Press. See Kiguli (2005). I would like to thank Susan Kiguli for allowing me to quote from her article.

4. Another indication of FEMRITE success is that Monica Arac de Nyeko, Doreen Baingana, and Jackee Budesta Batanda, all finalists for the Caine Prize for African Writing in the past few years, are also among its members. Baingana has published a cycle of short stories, *Tropical Fish: Stories out of Entebbe*, in the United States (2005).

5. At a national level, the country is recognizing the need for women's points of view to be represented. In compliance with the new constitution promulgated by President Museveni in 1995, a woman MP is elected for each of the 56 districts of Uganda. These women are listed in the *Uganda Districts Information Handbook* (2005).

6. Kyomuhendo has said that since childhood she has been interested in folklore and folk stories; she lived with her grandmother until she was 12, and it was from her that she learned most about the wisdom and traditions of her culture. Her grandmother followed strictly the rules of her culture, such as that which forbids married women to eat meat, and she knew a great deal about herbs and their medicinal properties.

7. The elders in Alinda's immediate family are not named because respect requires her to use only their familial titles: Mother, Father, Kaaka (grandmother). Other generic names, such as Nyinabarongo, indicate how labels may be used to rebuke women who have transgressed in some way; in time, these labels may replace a woman's given name. Thus, in Runyoro, a childless woman might be called "Engumba," a widow "Omufakati," and a woman who is too ambitious or self-reliant "Nakyeyombikire" (which means, literally, the one who builds her own house). When Alinda refers to the man who steps on a landmine simply as "the old man," she is again being respectful.

8. The "Center" does not indicate a town, but rather a road-side row of small shops that also forms a place where men would go to be sociable in the evening.

9. Knappert says that this grouping is still much debated by linguists, but he gives the groups as Bantu, Central Sudanic, Nilotic, Nilo-Hamitic, and Kalenjin; another source gives them as Bantu, Central Sudanic, East Nilotic, and West Nilotic (Pirouet 1995). The Bantu speakers, the largest group, live south of a line that can be drawn roughly from the northern end of Lake Albert in the west to Mount Elgon in the east. Both Luganda and Runyoro fall into this group. Kiswahili, which began centuries ago as a trading pidgin on the East African coast and has grown into a full language with many native speakers there, is an exotic language in Uganda (see note 14).

10. *Ebino* comes from the Runyoro word for teeth, "amaino," and, because of the prefix "eb," can loosely be translated as "bad teeth" or even "killer teeth." When these teeth have not yet erupted and the gum is swollen and possibly infected, the tooth buds are believed to be rotting and the cause of a baby's diarrhea, vomiting, and fever. Therefore the tooth buds are extracted, as is done to Alinda's baby brother. This condition is believed to be a result of bewitchment, and suspicion usually falls on foreigners. For the Western medical view of *ebino*, including the observation that when the extraction is done in crude conditions with unclean tools there is a grave danger of infection and other commplications, possibly leading to death, see Iriso et al. (2000).

11. The current fighting in northern Uganda has displaced almost as many people as the disaster in Darfur, Sudan. It is reported to threaten the re-building of South Sudan and to have embroiled the Democratic Republic of Congo ("Africa's Most Wanted" 2006: 42). African novels that reflect the transnational nature of civil war on the continent are discussed by Rogers (2005) and Tam-George (2005).

12. Provoked by Amin's earlier annexation of the Kagera Salient, Tanzania invaded Uganda in 1979, together with the Uganda National Liberation Army (UNLA), an umbrella organization of rebel forces. Tanzania's president, Julius Nyerere, believed that Obote was a fellow socialist and so had given shelter and assistance to the Ugandan rebels who operated from his country.

13. Goretti Kyomuhendo told me that, in her culture, the dove has at least three songs attributed to it, each of them shaped by the bird's singing all day without cease. Besides the song in the text, one is a lament in which the dove sings of a man's having cut off the branch of a tree in which it had its nest, a nest with eggs in it; in the other, the dove's endless repetition is mimicked to warn children, for example, to get up and do something rather than being bored, or being boring, like the dove. My thanks to Goretti for this and many other explanations of cultural matters, and my thanks to The Feminist Press for making it possible for me to go to Uganda and have the pleasure of learning a little about its cultures.

14. Unlike Kenya and Tanzania, Uganda has not adopted Kiswahili as its national language and, particularly in the south, continues to use either Luganda or English, or both, as the medium of communication. This is partly

because Kiswahili is so strongly associated with the rule of Idi Amin. He came, as the novel tells us, from Arua in the north where the Kakwa people live, but he grew up, during the British colonial period, in a military barracks where the lingua franca was Kiswahili. As this was his chosen language, and as his grasp of English was poor when he first came to power, Kiswahili continued to be the language of his army and so is linked primarily with brutal oppression in the minds of most Ugandan people. Attitudes are changing as the countries of East Africa experience greater stability. For example, Ssewakiryanga and Isabirye point out that since 1997 Ugandan artists have been going again to Nairobi to record their music, and that an album called *Yerere* by the Ugandan Richard Kawesa "could be described as the beginning of Swahili songs on the Ugandan popular cultural scene" (2006: 71).

15. While Nyinabarongo speaks with confidence about traditional knowledge and is always ready to relate the stories that contain this wisdom, it is clear that the war is jeopardizing cultural continuity. Had she, a somewhat suspect outsider, not been allowed to join Alinda's family group there would, after Mother's death, have been no one to take over this function. Kaaka and Nyinabarongo represent what Megan Biesele discusses as "sapiential authority," which she suggests is characteristic of egalitarian groups, while the destructive soldiers represent a distortion of structural authority that is found in hierarchical societies (Biesele 1993: 44).

WORKS CITED

"Africa's Most Wanted." 2006. *The Economist*, June 3, 42.

Baingana, Doreen. 2005. *Tropical Fish: Stories out of Entebbe*. Amhurst, MA: University of Massachusetts Press.

Barthes, Roland. 1974. *S/Z*. (trans. by Richard Miller). New York: Hill and Wang.

Beti, Mongo. 1971. *The Poor Christ of Bomba*. London, Ibadan, Nairobi: Heinemann.

Biesele, Megan. 1993. *Women Like Meat: The Folklore and Foraging Ideology of the Kalahari Ju/'hoan*. Bloomington and Indianapolis, IN: Indiana University Press.

Bukenya, Austin. 2000. "Introduction to Ugandan Literature." In *Ugandan Creative Writers Directory*. Kampala: Alliance Francaise, FEMRITE, New Vision, x–xix.

de Nyeko, Monica Arac. 2005. "Strange Fruit." In *Seventh Street Alchemy: A Selection of Works for the Caine Prize for African Writing*. Johannesburg: Jakana.

Gikandi, Simon. 1984. "The Growth of the East African Novel." In G.D. Killam (ed.). *The Writing of East and Central Africa*. London, Nairobi, Ibadan: Heinemann, 231–46.

Hove, Chenjerai. 1988. *Bones*. Harare: Baobab Books.

Iriso et al. 2000. "Killer Canines: The Morbidity and Mortality of Ebino in Northern Uganda," http://www. Blackwell-synergy.com/doi/full/10.1046/j.1365 3156.

Isegawa, Moses. 2000. *Abyssinian Chronicles*. London: Picador.
Kiguli, Susan. 2005. "FEMRITE und die Rolle der Schriftstellerin in Uganda: Personliche Einsichten." In Susan Arndt and Katrin Berndt (eds.). *Kreatives Afrika: Schriftstellerinnen über Literatur, Theater und Gesellschaft*. Wuppertal: Petter Hammer, 243–64. Forthcoming as *World and Worlds: African Writing, Literature and Society*. Susan Arndt and Katrin Berndt (eds.). Trenton, Asmara: Africa World Press.
Knappert, Jan. 1987. *East Africa: Kenya, Tanzania and Uganda*. New Delhi: Vikas Publishing House.
Kyomuhendo, Goretti. 1996. *The First Daughter*. Kampala: Fountain Publishers.
——. 1998. *Different Worlds*. Kampala: Monitor Publications.
——. 1999. *Secrets No More*. Kampala: FEMRITE Publications.
——. 2002. *Whispers from Vera*. Kampala: Monitor Publications.
——. 2006. *Hare and the King's Crow*. Kampala: Net Media Publishers.
Mamdani, Mahmood. 1983. *Imperialism and Fascism in Uganda*. Nairobi, Ibadan, London: Heinemann Educational Books.
Mutibwa, Phares. 1992. *Uganda Since Independence: A Story of Unfulfilled Hopes*. London: Hurst & Co.
Okurut, Mary Karooro. 2000. "Uganda Country Report." In *Women and Activism: ZIBF Women Writers' Conference 1999*. Harare: Zimbabwe International Book Fair Trust, 75–77.
Oyono, Ferdinand. 1991. *Houseboy*. London, Ibadan, Nairobi: Heinemann.
Pirouet, M. Louise. 1995. *Historical Dictionary of Uganda*. Metuchen, NJ & London: Scarecrow Press.
Rogers, Sean, with Isabel Hofmeyr. 2005. "Papa AK47 or Lolita in Africa: Gender, Nation and Citizenship in Sousa Jamba's *Patriots*." *Scrutiny 2*, 10(2): 35–45.
Ssewakiryanga, Richard, and Joel Isabirye. 2006. "'From War Cacophonies to Rhythms of Peace: Popular Cultural Music in Post-1986 Uganda." *Current Writing* 18(2): 53–73.
Tam-George, Austin. 2005. "Ken Saro-Wiwa's Sozaboy and the Gamble of Anomaly." *Scrutiny 2*, 10(2): 24–34.
Uganda Districts Information Handbook: Expanded Edition 2005-6. 2005. Kampala: Fountain Publishers.
Wangusa, Ayeta Anne and Violet Barungi. 2003. *Tears of Hope*. Kampala: FEMRITE Publications Ltd.

LaPorte County Public Library
LaPorte, Indiana

The Feminist Press at the City University of New York is a nonprofit literary and educational institution dedicated to publishing work by and about women. Our existence is grounded in the knowledge that women's writing has often been absent or underrepresented on bookstore and library shelves and in educational curricula—and that such absences contribute, in turn, to the exclusion of women from the literary canon, from the historical record, and from the public discourse.

The Feminist Press was founded in 1970. In its early decades, The Feminist Press launched the contemporary rediscovery of "lost" American women writers and went on to diversify its list by publishing significant works by American women writers of color. More recently, the Press's publishing program has focused on international women writers, who remain far less likely to be translated than male writers, and on nonfiction works that explore issues affecting the lives of women around the world.

Founded in an activist spirit, the Feminist Press is currently undertaking initiatives that will bring its books and educational resources to underserved populations, including community colleges, public high schools and middle schools, literacy and ESL programs, and prison education programs. As we move forward into the twenty-first century, we continue to expand our work to respond to women's silences wherever they are found.

For information about events and for a complete catalog of the Press's 250 books, please refer to our web site: www.feministpress.org.